the merchant of menace

**Center Point
Large Print**

**This Large Print Book carries the
Seal of Approval of N.A.V.H.**

the merchant of menace

JILL CHURCHILL

CENTER POINT PUBLISHING
THORNDIKE, MAINE

This Center Point Large Print edition
is published in the year 2005 by arrangement with
William Morrow & Company Books, an imprint of
HarperCollins Publishers, Inc.

The text of this Large Print edition is unabridged. In other
aspects, this book may vary from the original edition. Printed in
Thailand. Set in 16-point Times New Roman type.

ISBN 1-58547-691-9

Library of Congress Cataloging-in-Publication Data

Churchill, Jill, 1943-
    The merchant of menace / Jill Churchill.--Center Point large print ed.
        p. cm.
    ISBN 1-58547-691-9 (lib. bdg. : alk. paper)
    1. Jeffry, Jane (Fictitious character)--Fiction. 2. Television journalists--Crimes
against--Fiction. 3. Single mothers--Fiction. 4. Suburban life--Fiction. 5. Chicago
(Ill.)--Fiction. 6. Christmas stories. 7. Large type books. I. Title.

PS3553.H85M47 2005
813'.54--dc22
                                                                    2005018256

To Larry, David B., Amy, David L., and Rose

the merchant
of menace

One

"I can't do it all. I'll be dead or in the loony bin before Christmas," Jane Jeffry whined. She and her best friend and next-door neighbor, Shelley Nowack, were sitting at Jane's kitchen table. The house smelled of freshly baked cookies and coffee and just a hint of wet dog. It was only five in the afternoon, but the clouds were low and heavy and it was as dark as midnight outside.

"Nonsense," Shelley said in the brisk tone that intimidated traffic cops, school principals, and bankers, but to which Jane had grown immune.

Jane put her head down on the table, face forward with her nose to a place mat. "No, no. My children will be given into custody of my mother-in-law," she mumbled into the quilted fabric. "And she'll tell them awful things about me and great things about their dead father and—"

"Jane," Shelley snapped, "get a grip. They're not babies anymore."

Jane made a noise like a hippo pulling its foot out of the mud and continued her litany of woes. "Mel's mother's coming to town for Christmas and she's going to hate me—"

"She's not going to hate you and all that matters is what Mel himself thinks of you," Shelley persisted. Mel was Jane's "significant other," as her daughter

Katie insisted on referring to him.

"—and I have new neighbors on the other side of my house I've never met but already don't like—"

Shelley reached out to pet Jane's head sympathetically, but drew back her hand when she realized Jane had streaks of cookie icing in her blond hair. "You need to get your roots touched up—and the green gunk washed out," Shelley said. "Maybe they'd clean Willard up, too. A nice family trip to the groomers."

Willard, the big yellow dog who was lurking under the table waiting for possible cookie crumbs and contributing the only unpleasant odor in the mix, growled as if in disapproval of Shelley's suggestion.

Jane's muffled voice was just short of a wail. "Who cares if I have green hair or a smelly dog who likes to roll in the snow? Nobody's going to even look at me. I'm just a cookie-making, fruit-compoting, house-cleaning, madly-shopping drudge with red food coloring under my fingernails and a vacuum cleaner bag full of dog hair. Willard's doing that weird midwinter shedding thing again."

Shelley got up and poured them both new cups of coffee. "How did you get yourself into all this?" she asked. "You're doing the cookie exchange party and the neighborhood caroling party as well, aren't you? Back-to-back. Friday night and Saturday afternoon. Not good planning, Jane."

Jane sat up, running her sticky hands through her sticky hair and grimacing. "What a good friend you are to remind me of those," she said. "I take full blame for the cookie exchange party. It was my own idea, long before I got stuck with the rest of it. But as I recall, you encouraged me when I was reminiscing about how nice it used to be when that dear old lady who lived on the corner had a cookie exchange and all the neighborhood women got together once a year."

"I did. And it's going to be fun, Jane. I told you I'd provide the wine and tea and coffee and the boxes for everybody to take their traded cookies home in. I've already got the boxes all stacked up and decorated."

Jane gave her friend A Look that would have curled the hair of a lesser person. "Right. All I have to do is clean and decorate my house and make tons of extra cookies to be eaten at the party."

Shelley gestured expansively with her coffee cup. "You'd have to do that anyway," she said breezily. "But how did the caroling thing happen to you?"

"It was that damned Julie Newton."

"I thought you liked Julie."

"I thought I did, too. Despite her dreadful perkiness and optimism. When she got her cookie party invitation, she came by—gushing like mad about what a terrific idea it was and how it would promote neighborhood unity and how clever I was. She turned my head, Shelley. She made me feel like Lady Bountiful."

"She's good at that," Shelley said. "She once got me to run the Trash and Treasure booth at the church bazaar and I thought for a while it was my own idea."

"And I'm a sucker for flattery," Jane admitted. "So, Julie went on about how great it would be to have this neighborhood caroling thing and then have everybody get together at somebody's house afterwards for a buffet dinner. Sounded good to me and I nodded and agreed, and added suggestions, because I thought she was volunteering to do the whole thing. Then, when she had me thoroughly hooked on the scheme, she mentioned that she, of course, was having her kitchen renovated from the studs out and although the contractor—that nice young Bruce Pargeter guy who put in my pantry shelves—had said he might be done by Christmas, she wasn't sure she could count on him making the deadline and—"

"—you volunteered to be hostess?"

Jane leaned back in her chair and sighed heavily. "God help me, I did! Or she volunteered me. I don't remember the gory details. It was sort of like a train wreck. One minute I was chattering along, every bit as perky as Julie, and the next minute I'd agreed to have the whole neighborhood in for a buffet dinner."

Shelley looked over the cookies cooling on clean pillowcases on Jane's kitchen counter. "Jane, what are these green things supposed to be?"

"Elves," Jane said drearily. "Little nasty Christmas elves. The cutter looked like an elf, but they blobbed out when they cooked."

"They look more like holly leaves—or a fungus growth," Shelley said.

Jane smiled weakly. "But they taste okay. Throw some on a plate and let's make ourselves sick on them. I couldn't possibly let anyone else see them."

"I can't move," Shelley said. "My feet are stuck to your floor."

Jane nodded hopeless acceptance of this criticism. "Corn syrup. I dropped the bottle and the lid came off. I've already washed the floor twice and Willard's licked up as much as he could. Just leave your shoes there."

"Thanks, but I'd rather have my shoes stick than my feet." Shelley tossed some cookies on a plate, her shoes making a sound like Velcro being pulled apart, and sat down across from Jane. She nibbled a cookie cautiously and smiled. "They do taste okay. So, tell me about Mel's mother and why she'll hate you."

"Because he's her only son. He's a successful detective, up and coming, all that. And I'm a widow with three children, one already in college, which is a dead giveaway that I'm older than he is."

"So?" Shelley said.

"So she's going to see me as a predatory old hag, trying to trap her dear boy."

"Jane, you don't know that. She's going to adore you. Well, if you get this disgusting kitchen cleaned up, that is. And do some major repairs to your hair."

Jane shook her head. "Nope, she's not. Mel's already said so."

"He told you this?" Shelley said with amazement.

"Not in so many words. But he keeps mentioning how he's sure she's going to like me and my family. And how he's told her how terrific I am and how he's really, *really* sure we're going to get along great. I can

13

tell he's desperately trying to convince himself of this."

Shelley frowned. "Oh, that doesn't sound good."

"It doesn't. The more a man reassures me that everything's going to be fine, the more suspicious I become. And he's almost to a fever pitch about how well his mother and I are going to hit it off."

"At least you don't have to have her around all the time, do you?"

"No, she's staying with Mel, of course. He'll bring her to the cookie party because I invited her. And Christmas Eve and Day because I've invited both of them. Other than that, I don't imagine I'll see much of her," Jane said. "Of course, I won't see much of him, either, but since I've gotten myself stuck with all this entertaining, I guess that would have been inevitable anyway."

"Jane, I think you're making too much of all this. All you have to do is make the extra cookies and clean up your house—"

"Both of which are significant hurdles, in case you hadn't noticed."

Shelley glanced around. "The house does have a hint of nuclear holocaust about it. But you can manage. And I'll help with the buffet. Paul might even help us get a good deal with caterers."

Shelley's husband Paul owned a chain of Greek fast-food restaurants. They were enormously successful and neither Jane nor Shelley had ever been able to figure out why. They were in agreement that the food served in the restaurants was inedible. Paul even admitted it but said his policy was "If it ain't broke, don't fix it."

"Not Greek," Shelley assured Jane. "But he's subcontracted for a lot of caterers."

"Would you trust a caterer who subcontracted for his food?" Jane asked.

Shelley thought for a minute. "You've got a point. All right, then. We'll do a couple presliced hams, a bunch of scalloped potatoes from a boxed mix with some decent cheese and some green and red peppers added, and we'll tell everyone to bring either a salad or a dessert."

Jane sighed again. "Shelley, you're a good woman. Now tell me what gifts to get my kids."

"You haven't done your shopping yet?" Shelley almost yelled.

"I know. I know. You had yours finished in August."

Shelley didn't deny it. "It's too late to even count on catalogs. Sorry, Jane, but you're on your own there. Gift certificates are nice," she added wryly.

"Life was so much easier when they could be thrilled with a Big Wheel or a huge new box of crayons and half a dozen coloring books. Easier and cheaper. Mike sent me a list of computer programs and games he wanted. I went and priced them and reeled back out of the store looking like a woman who'd been hit in the head with a shovel."

Shelley abandoned the topic. "So what were your other complaints? Something about the neighbors?"

"Oh, that's right. You and Paul were out of town when they moved in."

"I've been meaning to get over there and meet them," Shelley said. "What's wrong with them?"

"Nothing, I guess, if you'd grown up in Possum Hollow and were married to your half-brother."

"Hicks?"

"Oh, way beyond hickdom, Shelley. Way beyond. You should have seen the furniture going in. Stuff I'd be embarrassed to put out for the trash. A hideous rainbow plaid sofa that made my eyes water. Dining room chairs with fake gold legs and plastic covers on the seats. I hate being a snob—"

"I can see why," Shelley commented, glancing at Jane's hair.

"But the wife wears housedresses—the kind our grandmothers wore in the Depression—and I saw her once at the grocery store with her hair in pin curls. I haven't seen anyone do that for at least twenty years."

"Have you met them, or just gawked at them?"

"We've met, briefly. I took a tuna casserole and a salad over to them for dinner the first night they were here. The husband—Billy Something, Jones or Johnson, I can't remember which—wears cowboy boots, a deer-hunting hat. He made us come in the house and meet his wife."

"Us?"

"Suzie Williams was with me. She brought a dessert. He very nearly drooled on her."

Jane and Shelley's friend Suzie, who lived a couple

16

houses down the block, was a big, voluptuous platinum blond. A Mae West–looking woman, but much prettier and just as vulgar.

"Why wouldn't he drool over Suzie? It's a perfectly natural impulse for a man."

"Well, the poor wife was standing right there, for one thing."

"Was he nasty?"

"No, not nasty. Just sort of showed off like a kid trying to impress a teacher he's got a crush on. Had to tell us all about his alligator boots and how he 'knew the ol' boy what raised the 'gators hisself.' And he wanted us to admire their pictures they were hanging. Landscapes they'd bought in a vacant gas-station parking lot. Oh, well. Maybe they'll grow on me. It'll be a cultural experience, at the very least."

"What does he do, did he say?"

"He's retired."

Shelley looked surprised. "Oh? Older people?"

"No. He looks about forty."

"What's he retired from?"

Jane shrugged. "No idea. Making moonshine?"

As if she'd made a cosmic announcement, her last word was followed by a trumpet blast of Biblical proportions that shook the windows.

Two

Billy Joe Johnson ran out the front door and down the sidewalk to where his wife Tiffany was standing. Once again, she had her hair in pin curls, but with a woolen scarf on her head, peasant-style. She was wearing jeans, a lumberjack shirt, and a light jacket she was trying to keep overlapped in the front and cover her ears at the same time. She didn't have enough hands for both.

"Ain't it great, Tiff?" Billy Johnson shouted over the music. The raucous noise had resolved itself into a brass band recording of "Hark! the Herald Angels Sing."

Tiffany cupped her ear. "What? I can't hear you!"

Jane and Shelley came out onto Jane's front porch and Billy Joe waved cheerfully at them. Jane raised a limp hand in response as she and Shelley minced down the front steps to get a better look at the Johnsons' house. It was almost buried in Christmas decorations.

Four-foot-high lighted candy canes lined the driveway. A life-sized Santa in a sleigh with two extremely lifelike reindeer were to the left of the sidewalk, and a coven of evil-looking plastic elves even more revolting than Jane's cookie elves disported themselves to the right of the yard. Every window in the house had a lighted snowman, angel, or star shining from it and was outlined with twinkling lights on the outside. In fact, the entire structure of the house was strung with lights. The bushes were a psychedelic nightmare, flashing and pulsating in red and green lights.

Jane and Shelley exchanged horrified looks. Tiffany cupped both hands and bellowed into Billy Joe's ear, "TURN OFF THE MUSIC!"

He bounced off to the house to do her bidding and a moment later the sound was abruptly cut off, mid-trumpet. It was suddenly so relatively silent that Jane could hear her pulse in her ears. Or maybe she'd gone suddenly deaf, she thought, and that's all she'd ever hear again. Her own heartbeat.

She tested her voice. "Shelley? Why didn't you tell me about this?"

Shelley was shaking her head, as if to clear it. "I've been inside all day and came from my kitchen door across the driveway to your kitchen door. I had no idea! He must have been working on this all day long."

"It's—" Jane fumbled for a single word that would describe the Johnsons' house. "—amazing! Horrible and amazing."

Jane's front door flew open and two of her children came barreling out. Katie, Jane's sixteen-year-old daughter, came to a sudden stop and said, "Holy sh—oops. Sorry, Mom." Her eyes were as big as saucers as she stared at the sight next door. "I was on the phone with Jenny and there was this awful noise . . ." Her voice trailed off.

Todd, in seventh grade and just inching past his sister in height, came out behind her, looked at the house, and grinned. "Awesome!" he said.

Jane glanced down the street. Here and there porch lights had come on, and people were standing on their front steps, huddled in sweaters and coats, staring at the Johnsons' house. Somebody pointed to the roof, and Jane looked up, then clutched Shelley's arm. "Shelley, the roof—"

Atop the house, set up between the two front dormers, was an entire life-sized crèche. Joseph, Mary, baby Jesus, wise men, shepherds, two sheep, and a smallish camel who looked like he came from a different set. The figures were brilliantly hued plastic, lighted from inside. It was, beyond any doubt, the most ghastly thing Jane had ever seen.

Several cars had stopped in front of the house and their passengers were gawking at the display.

Billy Joe was gesturing at Jane and Shelley. "Y'all come take a look from the front," he bellowed.

It would have been surly to refuse. But they didn't hurry. As they reached the couple, Billy Joe reached out to shake Shelley's hand. He pumped it like a slot machine handle. "I'm Billy Joe Johnson and this here is my wife Tiffany Ann. Tiff to her friends."

"How do you do?" Shelley said, trying to gently extricate herself from his grip. "I'm—" She paused as if attempting to gather her wits and remember her own name. "I'm Shelley Nowack. I live on the other side of Jane."

20

"Leggo her hand, Billy Joe," Tiffany said. "Pleased to meetcha, Shelley. What do you think?"

"About what?" Shelley asked.

Tiffany laughed merrily. "Why, of the house, of course. Isn't it just the best thing?"

Shelley's mouth moved but no words came out. Jane stepped into the breach. "It's certainly—impressive. So many—things. And music, too. Oh, my."

It was a feeble attempt at courtesy, but Billy Joe and Tiffany accepted it as a compliment and beamed at each other.

A police car pulled into the Johnsons' driveway and the officer, a young woman with sleek blond hair in a tidy chignon at the back of her neck, got out and stared, bewildered, at the house for a long moment before approaching Billy Joe. "Hello there, folks," she said, her smile huge and astonished. "We got a call about a noise at this address."

Billy Joe introduced himself and the others and said, "That was just my sound system. I guess I had it set too loud. I'm a little deaf myself, so I didn't notice. But Tiff says I damned near blew out her circuits!" He laughed uproarishly at this witticism. "Don't it look great?"

Jane felt a sudden engulfing tide of something like tenderness. These people really thought they'd created a work of art. They were proud of it and expected everyone else to like it. "I think it's wonderful," Jane said in a sudden, well-intentioned burst of mendacity. "Just wonderful."

Billy Joe swelled with pride. Tiffany simpered. Shelley looked at Jane as if she were seeing her for the first time and was not able to quite take in the sight.

"Just keep the noise level down if you would, Mr. Johnson," the police officer said. "Merry Christmas, everybody." She got in her car and backed out of the driveway, shaking her head and smiling.

Billy Joe invited Jane and Shelley inside for some holiday punch. "And bring the young 'uns, too."

"I really can't," Jane said. "I have cookies in the oven that have probably burned up by now. And Shelley's helping me with the icing. Maybe tomorrow?"

When they got back to Jane's front door, Katie had disappeared, but Todd was still standing and muttering, "Awesome."

"Don't even think about it, Todd," Jane said. "We're not doing anything like that. A Christmas tree, a tasteful wreath or two, maybe a few lights on the tree outside. That's it!"

"But Mom, old thing, just think if there were two houses in a row just like it. And maybe Mrs. Nowack would make a third one." He cackled with laughter. "Super!"

They came inside and he bounded up the steps, yelling at Katie to get off the phone so he could call his friend Elliott to come over and look.

"You think it's 'wonderful'?" Shelley quoted in a voice of doom.

"No, it's hideous, but they were so proud of it," Jane

said, shivering. "And I suddenly felt like a mother duck trying to console two ugly ducklings. Oh, Shelley, what if they decide to live here forever? It's a rental house, but sometimes renters stick around for a long, long time."

Shelley considered the question for a moment. "We'll either have to kill them—or ourselves—or move away. Might be time to start thinking about condos."

Jane was rummaging in the fridge, trying to find something to fix for dinner, when the doorbell rang. She found a neighbor, Sharon Wilhite, standing on the porch. "Just wondered if you needed some help getting ready for your parties," Sharon said. "How did you get conned into giving two of them back-to-back?"

"I'm still trying to figure it out, Sharon. Come in and tell me what to fix for dinner," Jane said.

"No good on that, I'm afraid. I almost never cook," Sharon said, shedding her coat and following Jane to the kitchen. She was a short blond, a bit on the buxom side, but very stylish and meticulously neat. Jane would have guessed her age to be about thirty.

Sharon looked around the kitchen as if it were foreign territory. "I don't have the time or skill for cooking and usually eat out, but I'm good with drinks."

"Drinks!" Jane exclaimed. "I haven't thought beyond coffee!"

"I'll bring along some wine, then."

Jane didn't know Sharon well, in spite of several years of living a few doors away, but liked her anyway. She was one of the few independent, single, childless women in the neighborhood. She was an attorney who specialized in property law and commuted to work in Chicago, so she wasn't around a lot. Her income permitted her to have cleaning help, yard workers, and driveway shovelers in the winter. But she made an effort to be part of the small community, singing in the church choir and volunteering time for the city council when their concerns touched on her expertise.

"Stay for dinner?" Jane offered. "Nothing spectacular."

Sharon shook her head. "I've got Chinese carryout ordered. In fact, I better get home and watch for it. Sure you don't need napkins, tablecloths, silverware, or something else I don't have to cook?"

When Sharon had gone, Jane fixed the kids and herself sandwiches and macaroni and cheese for dinner, went on with her baking, and started the first of many loads of washing that needed to be done. Todd put a new bag in the vacuum cleaner, which he insisted on calling "the Big Suck," in preparation for a marathon session of cleaning the next morning. Katie pitched in by devoting a full phone-free hour to cleaning every inch of the guest bathroom. This kind of cooperation and thoroughness was so astonishing to Jane that she was tempted to stand and admire the miracle of it.

Jane's mother had once told her that daughters don't get to be a pleasure to have around until it's almost time to lose them and Jane was starting to see the truth in that. After a couple of years of constant tears, arguments, and raging hormones, Katie was gradually turning into a very nice young woman. And in less than two years, she'd be going off to college.

Pull yourself together, you sap, Jane told herself briskly. *You always turn into a blubbering wimp at Christmastime.*

It didn't help that Billy Joe Johnson had his music back on. The volume wasn't nearly so deafening, although Jane could hear every lyric distinctly inside her house and suspected that outdoors it was probably intolerable. Still, she hummed along with the familiar melodies as she finished up the last batch of date-roll cookies and started packing the day's culinary output into lidded plastic containers that were intended for shoes and sweaters but were perfect for cookie storage. The floor was still sticky. She had inadvertently added some flour to the icing in her hair.

About nine there was a knock on the kitchen door. Shelley's special knock. Jane opened the door and Shelley nearly fell in. "Paul's sister Constanza is on her way over to our house. May I hide here?"

"Sure, but I was getting ready to take a shower."

"Take a shower. Take a long soaky bath if you want. God knows you need it. I'll eat cookies, watch television, and let myself out when I see her leave."

"So you didn't come for my scintillating companionship?"

"You're kidding, right?" Shelley said, shedding her coat and boots. "Go bathe. Please!"

Jane took Shelley's advice and soaked luxuriously, using up a good deal of some expensive jasmine-scented bath salts she'd been saving for a special occasion. Today hadn't been special in any good way, but she needed a treat.

When she came back downstairs half an hour later, Shelley was gone and the kitchen was spotlessly clean. The floor shone, the appliances glittered, everything was put away and the dishwasher was humming along. Jane laughed out loud. Shelley just couldn't stand a mess, not even someone else's mess. A note on the small blackboard on the refrigerator door said, *You need more dishwasher soap and tile cleaner. I stole a dozen cookies. S.*

Jane drifted into the living room, combed out her hair while watching television, and nearly fell asleep on the sofa. It had been a long day. Tomorrow would be even longer. She dragged herself upstairs and cuddled down into her freshly washed sheets. After trying to read for a few minutes, she gave up and turned off the light.

But the room didn't get dark.

She sat back up, confused. Then she realized that one of her bedroom windows was on the Johnson side of the house and the blaze of light from their decorations illuminated her room as if it were broad daylight.

She staggered over and pulled down the shade. Not much help. She dragged the drapes across the window. That was a little better. She'd have to get new ones tomorrow that were heavily lined. Great. One more thing to do! Pretty soon she'd have to hire a secretary to keep track of all her boring, necessary errands.

Back in bed, Jane dropped off into sleep halfway through "O Come All Ye Faithful."

Three

Jane was up early the next morning and got a little more cleaning done before even waking Todd and Katie. The clouds had cleared and it was a brilliantly sunny day. *Rats,* she thought. This meant she had to let Katie drive to school. Katie had her learner's permit now and was mad to get her hands on a steering wheel at every opportunity, but the rule, so far, was that she could only drive on dry streets. Jane wasn't up to teaching her the rigors of snow or rain driving yet. Teaching Katie, however, was easier than it had been to teach Mike. For one thing, Jane had anticipated it with Katie. With Mike she'd always assumed his father would take this duty, but her husband had been killed in a car accident before driving lessons had been necessary.

Mike had been a curb-hugger, nearly nipping off a number of mailboxes and joggers before he learned where the car should be. Katie got the car in the right place on the road and didn't seem to have any urge to speed. But she complained constantly and bitterly about the car itself. Jane couldn't really blame her. The beat-up old station wagon really was a disgrace. It was ten years old now and had spent those years hauling innumerable car pools—little kids bouncing all over the backseat, bigger ones who dropped potato chips and gum on the carpet and periodically spilled soft drinks. The exterior hadn't fared much better and although Jane was pretty good at avoiding falling in the pothole at the end of the driveway, the pothole was turning into an ever-widening chasm that occasionally snagged the undercarriage. Jane was wondering if it might not be cheaper to buy mufflers by the dozen.

"I can drive today, can't I?" Katie said, bounding into the kitchen. "Oh, my gosh! What happened to the kitchen? It's clean!"

"Mrs. Nowack cleaned it for me last night as a surprise. A very nice surprise," Jane admitted.

"Wish I had friends like that," Katie said. "Wonder if I could persuade Jenny to clean my room."

"I wouldn't count on it. You remember I took care of Mrs. Nowack's dog for a whole week while they were out of town. Jenny might stick you with an even bigger payback. Todd! Hold it," she added as he came into the kitchen and headed for the refrigerator. "If you spill so much as a drop or crumb in here, you'll be grounded until you're of voting age."

He looked around in wonder. "Hey, it's clean in here!"

"You don't need to sound *that* amazed," Jane groused. She wondered if she ought to put a drop cloth under the table.

When she returned from getting Katie to school, Todd's car pool had picked him up and Jane was pleased to discover that he'd heeded her warning. The kitchen was still spotless except for a cardboard milk carton on the table. She gave Shelley a call, thanking her effusively for cleaning up for her.

"Oh, Jane, quit being so mushy. You know that my deepest, darkest secret is that I love to clean. Just don't let anybody else know. Need any more help?"

"No, I think I've got a handle on it. I've got lists of things to do all over the house."

"You and your lists!" Shelley laughed. Jane was a compulsive list-maker, often breaking a single job down into components so she had more items to check off to bolster her sense of accomplishment. Sometimes, when she did something that wasn't on the list, she added it for the sole purpose of striking through it.

"If I don't have my lists, I just sit in a stupor, wondering what I'm supposed to be doing," Jane said. "But now I've got to start marking things off. Talk to you later."

The caroling party was to be the next evening, so she had two days to prepare. Cleaning the house and getting out the holiday decorations were the first orders of business, but there was shopping and cooking to be done, as well as bill-paying, carpooling and all the other normal, time-consuming chores. She was looking for where the toilet brush had deliberately hidden itself when the doorbell rang.

Julie Newton stood on the front porch, staring at the Johnsons' house. She was so stricken by the sight that she didn't even notice when Jane opened the door.

"Decorative, isn't it?" Jane said.

Startled, Julie gasped, "I've—I've never seen anything quite like it."

"Come in before you freeze," Jane said.

Julie did as she was told, following Jane to the kitchen. "I have the most exciting thing to tell you," she said, shedding her coat and stocking cap, her fingers making dainty darting motions at her hair to fluff it. Julie Newton, Jane thought, would be cute all her life. She was the perky kind of woman who never seemed to age. Her eyes crinkled at the corners when she smiled, which was most of the time, and she was always in motion. Fluffing her hair, gesturing enthusiastically as she spoke, swinging a leg when she was seated, and almost bouncing when she walked. A regular bundle of energy.

Jane offered her coffee or tea. Julie chose tea and squealed with delight at the sight of the plate of cookies Jane set on the table. "How darling! Jane, you're so clever!"

That's how she gets people to do things they don't want to, Jane thought. *With flattery.*

"Uh—what are these green ones supposed to be?" Julie asked.

"Elves. Don't ask. What's your news?"

Julie jiggled around in her chair with delight. "Oh, Jane. It's so neat! You know who Lance King is?"

"Lance K— oh, yes, that 'action reporter' on television. What's so exciting? Did somebody bump him off?"

"Bump him off? Oh, Jane, you're joking, right? You're so funny!"

"What about Lance King?"

"Well, you know he does all those reports on unfair stuff. Crooked businesspeople and sham charity organizations and all? But he sometimes hosts the regular nightly news from special events."

"Yes, I know."

Julie was quivering with excitement and looked like she was about to explode with the thrill of it all. "Well, Jane. *We* are going to be his special event tomorrow night!" Her voice was almost a shriek of joy.

"What?" Jane asked, appalled.

"Yes, it's true. He's going to anchor the news from your house! From your very own house!"

"Oh, dear God . . ." Jane whimpered.

"Isn't it fabulous? I knew you'd be so excited."

"Julie, I don't think that's—" Jane started to bleat.

"No, don't thank me. It was a pleasure to do it. I just took myself in hand and said, 'Julie Newton, there's nothing to stop you. The worst that can happen is that he'll say no,' and so I just called the television station and they actually put me through to him. I told him about the neighborhood caroling party and even suggested it would be a nice change, to do a 'revealing' piece about something that went right instead of wrong. I told him all about the neighbors, what nice, interesting people they all are—"

"You told him all about us?" Jane asked.

The thought made her stomach hurt. She, and many others, thought Lance King was far and away the most obnoxious individual who ever got in front of a television camera. He was the expert at the surprise attack, taking a camera crew to some unsuspecting individual's home or place of business, shoving his way in, and asking 'Do you still beat your wife' questions and berating the victim, barely skirting FCC regulations on obscene language issues. If he'd really only taken on genuine crooks and rip-off artists, it might not have been so offensive. But as often as not, he was simply dead wrong in his accusations. He'd be back on a week later, making a patronizing apology that always managed to be every bit as insulting as the original interview.

According to newspaper accounts, the local station was always being hit with enormous libel suits, most of which they lost. Or more correctly, their insurance carrier lost. There had been an article only a month ago about the insurance carrier trying to drop the station's coverage, but the station had filed suit against the carrier, claiming it was the carrier's incompetent lawyers who were to blame. When it got to court, a judge had ruled in the station's favor. The newspaper reporter, mincing among the libel laws himself like a trained soldier in a minefield, managed to suggest, without saying so, that the judge was afraid of what Lance King might to do him if he didn't rule in the station's favor. The general manager of the television station had been quoted as saying that Lance King was the brightest star in their galaxy of fine reporters and they considered his reports an honorable and necessary public service . . . blah, blah, blah. In other words, he was a point grabber and, Jane suspected, would have been out on his ear if the insurance had been canceled.

And now darling, cute, bubbly, idiotic Julie Newton had blabbed to him about their block caroling party, no doubt told him interesting tidbits about the neighbors and, worst of all, invited the jerk to Jane's house.

"Julie," Jane said, sitting down across from her and fixing her with a bleak stare, "you have to uninvite him. I won't have the man in my house."

Julie quit bouncing in place for a minute. Then said, "Oh, Jane, another joke!" She wiggled like a happy puppy.

"I'm not joking, Julie," Jane said firmly. "You're going to have to call him back, explain that you failed to check with the hostess of the party in advance and she has now told you her house can't accommodate any more people—like him and his crew."

"Jane, I can't do that."

"You *must* do it. Otherwise I'm going to tell everyone the party after the caroling is canceled. Or you can have it at your house."

"No, I can't. I don't have a kitchen. I made some

changes and Bruce couldn't finish it all." Julie sat very still for a moment. "He knows your name and address. Lance King does. I'm sorry, Jane, but he asked where the party was so he could come by early in the day and set up cameras. If I tell him you won't let him in, it'll make him mad at both of us."

"I don't care if he's mad at me," Jane said.

"Are you sure?" Julie asked.

"What can I do?" Jane asked Shelley half an hour later. Shelley had responded instantly to Jane's frantic call for advice and sprinted across their driveways to chew the situation over. "Even if it hadn't been some-body obnoxious, Julie had no business inviting an out-sider to my house."

"No, she didn't, but the problem now is to get rid of him," Shelley said.

"If I refuse to let him come, he'll be insulted and angry and he's the last person in the world I want to make enemies with," Jane said. "On the other hand, it makes my stomach hurt to think about having him in my house. People will think I'm expressing some sort of approval of his appalling behavior."

"You could come down with a sudden, violent, and highly contagious disease," Shelley suggested.

Jane shook her head. "No, nobody'd believe it. And I'd just end up sticking someone else in the neighbor-hood with the same problem. And I wouldn't even be able to help them out because of my smallpox or cholera or whatever."

Shelley took a sip of her coffee. "Much as I like to be the neighborhood wise woman, always ready with a solution, I'm coming up empty on this one," she admitted. "How did you leave it with Julie?"

"You mean after I beat the stuffing out of her? I've never been so tempted to smack somebody upside the head. I told her I wanted an hour to think about it."

The doorbell rang and Jane found Bruce Pargeter standing on the front steps, looking very upset.

He introduced himself and Jane said, "I know you, Bruce. Remember, you put in new pantry shelves. Come in out of the cold."

"I remember. I wasn't sure you did."

Bruce was a chunky, florid-faced young man, probably about thirty years old, Jane would have guessed, who lived with his widowed mother at the other end of the block. He was a wizard at fixing, repairing, or renovating almost anything. Almost everyone in the neighborhood had benefited from his skills at one time or another. One of the advantages to having him around was that he was unfailingly cheerful and polite and had excellent taste. He could suggest to homeowners that their own ideas were dreadful without being the tiniest bit rude about it.

But today he didn't look the least bit cheerful. In fact, he looked extremely upset.

"Hi, Bruce," Shelley said when they entered the living room. "I've been meaning to tell you how happy I am with that flooring in the family room. I'm so glad you convinced me to get the planking rather than the squares."

"Too bad you don't have a tape recorder running, Bruce," Jane said with a laugh. "Not very many people have ever heard Shelley admit that someone else was right and she was wrong."

But Bruce Pargeter only gave her a thin smile. "Jane, I want to warn you about something and ask a favor. I'm doing Julie Newton's kitchen and I couldn't help but hear her on the phone this morning. Do you know she's invited Lance King to the neighborhood caroling party?"

"I'm afraid I do know. Shelley and I were just trying to figure out what to do about it."

Bruce gave her a grim look. "Jane, if you value the quality of your life, you won't let that—that person in your house. Believe me, you'll regret it the rest of your life. He's the most evil person in the world."

Four

It turned out that Bruce's experience with Lance King went way back to years ago in Kentucky, where they both lived at the time.

"Ever heard of karst topography?" he asked.

"Something to do with caves, isn't it?" Jane said.

Shelley looked surprised. "I never cease to marvel at the weird snippets of things you know about, Jane."

"College geology," Jane said. "I liked geology."

Bruce took up the explanation. "In the simplest terms, karst topography is where you have limestone bedrock below the soil. When there's a lot of groundwater, it erodes the limestone over time and that forms caves. If it erodes far enough, sometimes the top of the cave falls in and you get a sinkhole. Most of the middle part of the country is limestone bedrock, but only some areas get sinkholes. Kentucky is one of them."

"This has something to do with Lance King?" Shelley asked.

"Quite a lot," Bruce said. "My dad was a contractor outside Louisville. He built a little subdivision, eight or ten houses, and just as the last one was being completed, the first one fell into a sinkhole. The added weight of the house itself collapsed the ceiling of the cave and the entire house just collapsed into the hole."

"Oh, my gosh!" Jane exclaimed. "Shouldn't somebody have known there was a big hole under the house?"

Bruce nodded. "Oh, yes. Nobody in their right mind would build in that part of the country without having a thorough geologic survey done. My dad hired the people, who assured him that it was solid bedrock."

"I sense Lance King coming into the story real soon," Shelley said.

"Yep," Bruce said. "But it was much worse than just losing the building." His expression grew even more bleak. "It happened early in the morning while a woman and her two-month-old baby were in the house

37

asleep. They were both killed. Crushed as the house collapsed."

Jane and Shelley tried, unsuccessfully, to stifle their gasps of horror.

Bruce sighed. "I think my dad would rather it had been him. He nearly had a breakdown when he heard. It was only the old Puritan ethic of facing things down that kept him going. And, of course, that's where Lance King comes in. He was on his first job out of college, heard about the tragedy, and took out after my dad like a rabid wolverine. He did pieces on him almost every night for a week. Went around to other people Dad had built houses for, scaring them to death, working them all up to say Dad was a murderer—God, it was awful."

"Your poor family," Jane said softly.

"Lance knew from the beginning that the responsible party was the geological surveyors. But they were remote, no one local person to blame. Not one upstanding local citizen who was already nearly broken with grief and guilt. He sneaked around, getting unflattering pictures of Dad, showing them on the news, carrying on about the poor innocent baby . . . Well, you've seen him in action here."

"To my disgust," Shelley said.

"It made King's career. And utterly destroyed my father. His reputation went into the hole with the house and people. Somebody . . ." He paused and cleared his throat to get the next words out. "Somebody spat at him on the street."

Bruce's voice shook and his eyes shone with tears.

They were all silent for a moment, trying to absorb the awful humiliation. Finally Shelley asked, "That's why your family moved here?"

Bruce pulled out a big, ragged handkerchief and dabbed at his nose and eyes. "Dad had a sister and brother in Chicago. He and Mom moved up here—I finished college in Kentucky and joined them. He intended to start over, but his heart and spirit were broken. He was such a good, good man. When he got here, he had a nervous breakdown, was hospitalized for a while, and his health started failing. He died three years later."

"I think *my* heart is broken, Bruce," Jane said.

He was obviously embarrassed. "I'm sorry. I don't go around talking about this, but I thought you should know and I'd be glad if you didn't mention this to anyone else. It's downright dangerous for Lance King to even know who you are. He's always on the lookout for someone to destroy. And he's an expert at it. Makes himself look like a crusader for all that's right and good while perfectly innocent people have their lives torn to shreds. He killed my father. It was a long, tortured death."

"That does it, Shelley. Lance King is pure scum and it would pollute my home to let him in," Jane said, knowing she was sounding melodramatic and not caring.

Shelley said mildly, "It's going to make him come

down on you and Julie, you know."

"Shelley, are you saying I'm wrong to take this stand?"

"Absolutely not. I'd do the same, but you do need to consider the possible consequences."

"I don't care what kind of trouble Julie gets into. It's her fault to begin with. And there's nothing he can do to me. I have no dark secrets." She smiled. "Sometimes I wish I did. I'd be so much more interesting."

"Jane, Bruce's father didn't have dark secrets either," Shelley reminded her. "There's nothing to stop Lance King from simply making up something."

Jane sat down, deflated. "I know that. But it's a matter of principle. Bruce is right: Lance King is evil. Deliberately, coldly evil. I couldn't betray someone as nice as Bruce by letting the man in the house and appearing to approve of him. I'm going to call Julie before I waver."

Julie was crushed by Jane's ultimatum. Her voice wavered and she was near tears, but she agreed to call and cancel the Lance King visit. It was only ten minutes later that Julie called Jane back, bubbling and cheerful. "It's all right. He took it really well, Jane. Said he understood that a television crew was a big imposition at the last minute."

Jane was stunned. "You actually spoke to him and he said that?"

"Yes, he was very considerate and understanding. I'm so relieved. I'm really sorry I acted without thinking and got us into this mess, but it's all worked out now."

Jane hung up the phone, more alarmed than ever. This didn't sound like Lance King at all. And Jane simply couldn't buy the concept that he was secretly a considerate gentleman. But what could she do? He'd backed off, taken himself out of the picture, ceased to be a problem.

Yeah, right, she told herself. *In a pig's eye.*

Jane spent the rest of the morning and half the afternoon getting out the Christmas decorations. The bottle-brush plastic tree was the first item. She hated having a plastic tree, but the real ones gave her hives. She dragged its assorted parts out of the big cardboard box in the basement, set it up, and then tackled the lights.

Strings of Christmas lights were mysterious and frustrating things. Every January when she put them away, she wound each strand separately, put a rubber band around it, and wrapped it in tissue paper. And every year, when she got them back out, they were in a hopeless snarl. During the summer they must have been doing wicked and vaguely obscene things with each other. Either that or Max and Meow, her two cats, entertained themselves playing in the box—which was much more likely but less fun to contemplate.

The next step was the tree ornaments. This always made her maudlin. Every ornament meant something dear to her. Among her favorites, there were the balls covered with glitter that Mike had decorated when he was a first-grader; the paper chain of rapidly disintegrating snowmen holding hands that Todd had cut out; the tiny china bride and groom her mother had sent the first year Jane was married; the miniature, fragile Swiss clock Shelley had given her; and the bird nest.

That one really made her weepy. The year Jane's husband had died, her honorary uncle Jim had declared that the children needed a real tree, Jane's hives notwithstanding. He promised her he'd put it up and take it down and she'd never have to touch the thing. They bundled up the kids and Jim drove them to a tree farm where they found a tree with an abandoned bird nest. It was carefully woven and held together with mud. Uncle Jim had made an uncharacteristically sappy remark about Jane and her baby birds that reduced her to tears then—and every time she got the bird nest out since then.

She so dearly loved the older man who had been a lifelong friend of her parents and had served as their substitute when she was widowed. Her father was with the State Department and had been helping to negotiate a treaty in a small African community that was unreachable by phone the week Steve died. But Uncle Jim, retired career army, second career Chicago cop, stiff as a poker and tough as nails, had been there for her.

She wiped away her tears and finished putting up the ornaments, then moved on to setting up the little manger scene. The kids had loved to play with the scene when they were little. The lambs had lost their little ceramic ears, baby Jesus had a crayon mark on His arm, and one of the wise men's camels had lost a leg years ago, which Jane had glued back a bit crookedly. The camel now stood in what looked like a drunken slouch with the wise man poised to fall off. The thatch on the roof of the manger had gradually disappeared in packing, unpacking, and being played with. But she'd never replace it with a respectable-looking new version.

The nutcracker figures were lined up on the mantel—it was supposed to be bad luck to put them away, but Jane always did so anyway. She got out the punch bowl and Christmas cups, the felt tree skirt her mother-in-law Thelma had made when Jane had Mike. Jane had always taken this gesture to mean that Thelma had acknowledged (grudgingly) that, having given birth to the first Jeffry grandchild, Jane was finally part of the family.

She filled the Santa bowl with candy canes, stuck the artificial wreath made of tiny foil packages on the refrigerator door, and set out the red and green candles all over the house. Mike could set up the train and miniature village when he got home from college. It had always been his special job and he guarded it jealously. She hung the red tapestry stockings she'd gotten at the church craft sale the year before, put out the Christmas afghan, and stood back to admire her handwork. As if it were a signal, music started blasting from next door.

"O Little Town of Bethlehem" at 100 decibels.

She sighed heavily. Her activities had put both the dreaded Lance King and her very odd new neighbors out of her mind for several hours. Now reality and the present intruded and she went back to fretting about what the next couple days might hold in store.

Five

Jane ran out and did some more of her shopping and dashed home before Todd could get back from school and snoop into packages. As she turned onto her block, she saw a familiar little figure plodding along the street on her way home from the school bus stop. Jane pulled the station wagon to the curb, opened the window, and said, "Hop in, Pet. You look cold. I'll drop you at your house."

"Thank you very much, Mrs. Jeffry, but I'll walk. My father says I can't get in other people's cars," Pet Dwyer said precisely.

"I'm sure he meant strangers' cars, dear, and I'm not a stranger. But it's good advice. See you later."

She was still shaking her head and chuckling when she pulled into the driveway. Shelley was just coming out to get her newspaper and followed Jane into Jane's house. "What are you grinning about?" she asked. "Did you win the lottery? Inherit fabulous jewelry from a long-lost aunt? Is your mother-in-law going on an around-the-world cruise for a year?"

"No, nothing that good. I just offered that little Pet Dwyer a ride and she turned me down because she can't accept rides. She's such a weird little girl. I've got to hide Todd's presents before he gets here."

Jane disappeared into the basement for a moment and when she returned, Shelley asked, "Pet Dwyer?"

"Patricia, really. You know her, Shelley. Lives across the street and two or three houses down? The blue house with the white trim. She comes over at least three times a week to visit Todd."

"Oh, yes. Todd likes her? Are they a 'thing'?"

"I don't think Todd knows what to make of her. She's so bright and prim and grownup-talking. Like a very smart but repressed Victorian child. She doesn't drool over him, so he's not scared of her like he would be of any other girl. And she seems to genuinely like the same things he does. One day she brought over a microscope and a bunch of rather revolting slides of things like ant feet and fly wings. Nothing could have charmed him more. He's really not interested in girls yet, even though it's macho to pretend he is, and is sort of embarrassed at having one follow him around."

Shelley nodded. "I heard my son and his friends using an extraordinarily rude word the other day for a part of the female anatomy. I eavesdropped for a bit and discovered they thought it meant a girl's hairdo. I explained, as tactfully as possible, that it didn't mean that and I would wash out the mouth of any child who said it in my house again."

"Did you tell them the real meaning?"

"Good Lord, no! Imagine if they went home and told their parents that Mrs. Nowack was educating them in gutter language."

At that moment Todd came slamming into the house. "Mom, help me! That Pet is on her way here. I saw her coming down the street."

"I can't save you. Into each life some Pets must fall."

"Mom, I'm serious! She saw me come in the house. What'll I do?"

"You'll be nice to her," Jane said mildly. "Let her play with your hamsters."

"Every time she touches them she has to wash her hands afterwards like she was getting ready for surgery! Oh, okay. Okay."

Pet was at the front door a few minutes later. "That house next door to yours is rather garish, isn't it, Mrs. Jeffry," she said. She made it sound as if it just might be Jane's fault.

"Garish," Jane said. "Yes, excellent word for it. Come in, Pet. Todd's just gone up to change his clothes. Come in the kitchen and have some milk and cookies with Mrs. Nowack and me."

"I can't eat sweets because I didn't bring along my toothbrush," Pet said. "But thank you anyway. I'm sure they're very good. And I can't drink milk from the grocery store. My father has special milk delivered."

"Soy or something, I guess," Jane said. "You know

46

what? I have lemonade and also extra toothbrushes that haven't even been unwrapped. You can have a cookie *and* a toothbrush," Jane said, wondering how a real live child could be this proper and noble. She needed to be tickled or something.

"Thank you so much, Mrs. Jeffry."

Her eating was as prissy as her speech. She munched the cookie in little rabbity nibbles, holding a napkin at chest level to catch any crumbs. Jane knew Pet was in seventh grade with Todd, but she was one of the late bloomers. Gangly, flat-chested, and looking like she had a larger person's teeth filling her mouth, she was still a knobby-kneed little girl. Jane could remember some of Katie's friends at the same age looking like twenty-five-year-old models. Or at least giving it a good try. But Pet, with her bottle-bottom glasses and tightly braided hair, had a long way to go and didn't appear to be in any hurry.

"It must take your mother ages to braid your hair every morning," Jane said as she poured Pet a glass of lemonade.

"I don't have a mother. She died in a car wreck."

"Oh, Pet. I'm so sorry," Jane exclaimed. "I had no idea."

"It's okay. I was little. I don't remember her, not exactly. But I have lots of pictures of her. My father braids my hair."

Jane was saved from asking any more inadvertently awkward questions by Todd. "Oh, hi, Pet," he said as if he were surprised to find her there. "What's up?"

47

"My dad gave me a computer program about pyramids," Pet said. "I thought you might like to see it. You can build a sarcophagus with it and move treasures around inside to foil grave robbers and wrap up mummies."

"Do you want me to load it on my computer in the basement?" Jane asked. She had a small office in the basement where she worked on what she'd come to think of as the Endless Novel. She estimated that it was three-quarters done and was going to really, *really* work on it after the holidays. She remembered thinking the same thing last Christmas. But at least she was two hundred pages farther along now than then.

"I know how to load programs, Mrs. Jeffry. I just hope you have enough RAM."

For some reason, Pet's behavior made Jane want to be a child *for* her. Show her how it was done. She nearly said, *"Ram, schram, bippity bam"* with a girlish laugh, but forced herself to reply only, "I don't know, Pet. Can you tell when you turn it on?"

"Is it an old computer?" Pet asked.

"No, only about two or three years old."

Pet allowed herself a slight smile. "That's very old for a computer."

"Then you may use my laptop. It's only a few months old. It's downstairs, too."

Pet and Todd went down the basement stairs and Jane quietly closed the door behind them. "Oh, dear. Poor little thing," Jane said to Shelley. "At least she

48

forgot about brushing her teeth. I guess there's hope for her."

"You never know," Shelley said. "She could get a figure and contacts and take down her hair someday and turn into a blues singer in a slinky purple-sequined dress."

Jane shook her head. "No, I think she's going to get stronger glasses and go around in a lab coat with a pocket protector."

"Pocket protector! Oh, I know who she is now," Shelley said. "There was a Sam Dwyer sitting in the hall with me waiting to see the teacher at the same time I was last week. A real, live grown-up geek of the first order. Not really too bad-looking, but the tidiest man I've ever met. Real short hair, glasses as thick as Pet's, and a very narrow tie that he must have been babying along since the seventies. I tried to make conversation with him, but it was heavy going. He simply didn't want to talk to me."

"Imagine!" Jane said, grinning.

"I was irritated," Shelley admitted. "I was just curious about him and he wouldn't tell me anything about himself."

"Sounds like both of them need to hang out with a blues singer in a slinky purple-sequined dress."

Shelley took another cookie. "These things are addictive," she complained. "It's a shame they're so ugly. Now that I think about it and have met little Pet, I'm even more curious."

"You're as nosy as Lance King," Jane said.

Shelley drew herself up indignantly. "But my motives are pure, unlike his. I don't want to wreck people's lives, just know about them. And maybe be helpful. There aren't that many single men in the neighborhood and I thought maybe Suzie Williams—"

Jane yelped with laughter. "Suzie Williams? He doesn't exactly sound like Suzie's type!" She was the one who'd accompanied Jane to meet the Johnsons, and she made no bones about wanting to get out of selling lingerie at the local department store via marriage to a man who could support her in style.

Shelley said, "Suzie's 'type' of man is anyone with decent table manners and a balanced checkbook with lots of lovely money in it. Or so she claims."

"I think it's all a facade. I think Suzie wants to be in love," Jane said. "You'll see. Someday she'll fall head over heels with a dashing but unemployed race-car driver with long hair and a dazzling come-hither smile. Sort of like that sexy World War One guy in the pizza ad."

"You don't think she's the one to bring the Dwyers, father and daughter, into the human race?" Shelley asked.

"I think she'd scare them to death. I imagine *you* scare them."

"I only scare people when I need to," Shelley said smugly.

Jane opened the basement door, listened for a moment, nodded approval of what she heard. "Want more coffee?" she asked Shelley.

"I wouldn't object violently. Where do you stand on the Lance King thing?"

"Oh, I forgot to tell you. Julie called this morning and said she'd uninvited him and he took it like a man."

They were both silent for a moment while Jane refreshed the coffee cups. "I don't believe it," Shelley said when Jane sat back down.

"I believe he said it," Jane said, frowning. "But I don't believe he meant it. I'll bet he's down at city hall or the newspaper files or someplace else trying to dig up something to ruin me with. He's not going to find anything. I've got plenty of sins on my soul, but I don't believe any of them are public record."

Jane's son Mike came home from college that evening. He wasn't due to come home until the next day, but cheerfully explained that he'd come sooner so he could set up the electric train. Jane opened her mouth to object, but remembering the classes she'd cut in college for far less valid reasons, said nothing.

"What's happened to the house next door?" Mike asked when he'd dragged his belongings into the house and dumped them in the living room.

"New neighbors," Jane said. "They're really into decorating for the holidays in a big way. Be sure and take your things upstairs right now. We have to keep the house really clean for a couple days. There's a neighborhood caroling party tomorrow night and everybody's coming here afterwards. And the next afternoon I'm having a cookie party. Then we can slob out until Christmas Eve when your grandmother's coming to dinner."

"A cookie party. That's great. I remember you used to go to those parties when I was a little kid," Mike said. "We ended up with all kinds of good stuff. Remember those stained-glass cookie things? Let's make some of those."

"Pick up some Life Savers and gingerbread mix next time you're out and we will."

"How about tonight? I haven't had dinner and want to go pick up a hamburger," Mike said. "Where are Todd and Katie? I'll take them along."

Jane bellowed up the steps for the other kids and watched the reunion of the siblings. The younger two were of ages that couldn't openly show affection for a big brother, but they were obviously glad to see him.

Katie gave him an air kiss.

"Hey!" Todd said when Mike gripped him in a bear hug. "What's with the mushy stuff? You were just here at Thanksgiving."

"Yeah, but I didn't have presents with me then. Help me take my junk upstairs."

Katie trailed along after them, pretending that she was going that direction anyway. Jane caught a snatch of the conversation and called after them, "Katie, quit asking about Mike's friends. You are *not* in the dating market for college boys."

"Oh, *Mother!*"

Jane stood in the middle of her still-clean kitchen. Lance King didn't matter, the scratchy blare of a reggae version of "We Three Kings" blasting from next door was of no consequence. The fact that she had to feed at least thirty people this time tomorrow wasn't even much of a concern. She had her kids home and they were pretty neat kids.

Life didn't get much better.

Six

But life could—and did—get considerably worse the next day.

It started with the anonymous note stuck into the front storm door. Jane noticed it as she came in from getting the morning paper. Handwritten and copied on bright pink paper, the note was signed *A Group of Concerned Neighbors.*

In Jane's experience a "group" with no name attached usually meant one disgruntled, cowardly individual.

The gist of the note was that the Johnsons' Christmas display was a detriment to the neighborhood. It created noise and light pollution. "Light pollution?" Jane snorted out loud. Furthermore, the Concerned Neighbor went on, it would create a traffic problem as word spread and more and more people came to look at it, thus endangering the welfare of the children who might not be used to so many cars on the street and possibly drawing the attention of a lot of "less than desirable" outsiders. Moreover, the Group of Concerned Neighbors said, going overboard on political correctness, the display was largely Christian in intent and was offensive to Jewish, Moslem, and atheist residents. It might, the Group said, even violate the constitutional right to separation of church and state.

Jane stared at the note and muttered angrily, "Get a life!" as she headed for the phone. When Shelley answered, Jane said, "Have you opened your front door yet? No? Do so. I'll wait."

It took Shelley a surprisingly long time to return. "Assholes," Shelley said, rattling paper furiously.

"What took you so long?" Jane asked.

"I ran out to the sidewalk to see if the perps of this trash were still on the street. They weren't."

"I could have told you that. This is a 'dark of the night' communication."

"So what do we do about it?"

"Well, we certainly don't want to violate any constitutional rights," Jane sneered. "But there's a section urging neighbors to call city hall and make their feelings known. I suggest we organize people to do just that. I'll call the people on this side of the block, you call the other side."

Before she called any neighbors, she called city hall herself. She gave her name and address and said, "I'd like to make known my feelings about the house decorations next door to me."

"Yes?" the city clerk said wearily. "I've gotten several calls."

"I like the decorations." This was an outright lie, but Jane's constitutional rights provided for free speech, which included lying for a good reason, she figured. "And I like the Johnsons. And I dislike the mean-spirited jerks who put this note in my door."

There was a brief silence, then the clerk said, much more cheerfully, "Thank you, Mrs. Jeffry. I'll see that your comments are passed up the line."

Jane called Suzie Williams next, who said, "I'm just on my way to work, Jane, but I'll call the city clerk when I get there. That house looks like a combination of Disneyworld and a train wreck, but it's their house and the Nazi busy-bodies haven't got any damned business interfering."

"Hey, Suzie, before you go, do you happen to know Sam Dwyer? Down the block. Single. Has an owlish-looking little girl?"

"You bet I do," Suzie said with a rich chuckle. "Gotta go spend another fulfilling day stuffing little old ladies into corsets. Tell you about him later."

Jane got out her address book and called everyone else on her side of the block that she knew. Two of them tried to convince her that the note was perfectly correct and Something Must Be Done. Another two were as outraged as she and thanked her for suggesting they call the city offices. The rest were either neutral or not answering. She thought she'd won over a couple of the neutral parties.

Her last call was to Sharon Wilhite. "Not to worry," Sharon said. "It would take years of legal wrangling to impose somebody else's standards on the Johnsons. Since they're renters, only their landlord could· stop them."

"I wonder who the owner of the house is?" Jane said.

"Me," Sharon said with a laugh. "I bought it as rental property a couple years ago. And I don't much like people trying to use the Constitution to be rude. I'll call the city before I go to work and make sure they know it's okay with me."

Jane hung up. "Constitutionalize this!" she said, wadding the pink paper up and throwing it in the trash. Then she fished it back out and left it on the counter so that the Concerned Citizen, who was sure to be one of her guests this evening, would see what her opinion was.

She suddenly realized that she hadn't ever invited the Johnsons to the party. That was *really* rude, having a block party next door and ignoring them. She didn't have a telephone number for them, so she threw on a coat and boots and went next door. Though she could hear a television newscast, it took a long time for anyone to answer the doorbell and she was about to give up when Tiffany opened the door. "Oh, Miz Jeffry, come on in," she said. She was wearing a new-looking, but tacky robe—fluorescent pink with little white bobbles outlining the yoke.

Jane followed her into the house and they were just

sitting down as the sound of a computer printer started up. Tiffany looked startled, then trotted to a door at the back of the living room and said, "Billy, Miz Jeffry's here to visit." She shut the door firmly. "Billy plays them computer games and sometimes prints out hints and stuff," she said.

Why's she explaining? Jane wondered. And then had the realization that Tiffany was lying. Billy was printing out something else entirely. She was sure of it. Maybe someone had put the Concerned Neighbor note on their door, too, and he was writing a rebuttal to pass out.

Jane explained about the neighborhood caroling party and suggested tactfully that the Johnsons join the others and perhaps could turn off their own sound system tonight. "It's hard enough for some of us to carry a tune at all, without hearing something else at the same time," she said. "Then everybody's coming to my house for a supper. Nothing fancy."

"That's real nice, Miz Jeffry—"

"Please, call me Jane."

"Okay, Jane. Can I bring something to the dinner? I could do up some hog jowls and beans. Or a mess of beets—?"

"No," Jane said more forcefully than she intended. "I've got everything taken care of. All we need is you and Billy to join us."

"We'd be proud to," Tiffany said.

In for a penny, in for a pound, Jane thought dismally. "Then tomorrow, I'm hosting a cookie party and I'd like for you to come to that, too. Just you. It's a girl thing."

"What's a cookie party?"

"Everybody brings two dozen of their best cookie recipe," Jane explained. "All the plates are put out and then everyone goes around and chooses two dozen of other people's cookies. That way, everyone goes home with a nice variety. Sometimes the ladies make up pretty little recipe cards to go with their contribution. But you don't have to. Some like to keep their recipe a secret and that's okay."

"Oh, Mi— Jane, what a nice neighborly idea. I'd love to come. I got a real good recipe for my granny's tarts. That's okay, isn't it, if they ain't exactly cookies? Or maybe I could make some of them little fluffy things."

Jane had visions of bottled marshmallow dip slathered on graham crackers. "That's fine, Tiffany. Just so it's not a cake or pie that has to be cut. Now I better get going. I've got a lot to do today."

Jane was as good as her word. Purse-sized notebook in hand, she started with the grocery store. She'd been so compulsive that she had several lists. First, the list of dishes she was serving, with the ingredients as sub-headings, then she'd rearranged the individual items into shopping aisles so she wouldn't have to go back for celery when she already had the onions. *I'm so well organized,* she preened silently, *Shelley would be proud.*

She was able to get her groceries in record time and

even made it home before the bags of ice started melting. To her surprise, Mike was awake, dressed, and watching for her. He brought in the bags of food and put the ice in the basement freezer while she set everything out in the order she was going to need it. "Mike, I need a favor. I have two hams ordered and ready to be picked up. I've already paid for them. Could you run and get them from the ham shop?"

While he was gone, she started cooking. She filled several disposable aluminum pans with packaged scalloped potato mix, added thinly sliced red and green pepper rounds, and topped them off with extra cheese. No room in the fridge for them until it was time to put them in the oven, but she'd cleared a space in the garage, put down brown paper, and they could sit there under foil keeping cool until later. She threw together the five-bean salad, tossed it with the dressing, and added the big bowl to the garage stash of food.

The cats were charmed by this unusual activity. Jane noticed them watching her and laid a cardboard box over the food.

When Mike returned with the hams, she asked him to take them to Shelley's. "They're going in her oven this afternoon since I don't have room," she explained. "Oh, and take along the parsley to decorate the plates. God, I'm good, aren't I?"

Feeling devastatingly domestic and terribly smug, Jane took on the dining room. She'd already struggled to get all the table extensions put in place, which hardly left room to squeeze around the end of the table, and had put the big red tablecloth and centerpiece in place. Now she put out the sturdy paper plates (she'd sprung for far more than was sensible for them because she loved the colorful wreath pattern around the edges), cups, and plastic silverware. She fished around in the drawers of the china cabinet for hot pads and scattered them artistically.

Jane closed the door on the dining room after a last, admiring look, to keep the cats and Willard out of the room, and she tackled the broccoli.

"Anything I can do?" Mike asked, coming in the kitchen door. "By the way, Mrs. Nowack said parsley is passé and she's doing a pineapple and Chinese mustard sauce for the ham."

"Parsley is passé? How dare she?" Jane said with a grin. "I'm the hostess with the mostest today."

"Be careful," Mike said, pouring himself a soft drink and sitting down at the table.

"Of what?"

"Of getting too cocky."

Jane went on cutting broccoli flowerettes. "Are we talking about me or you?"

"Me, I guess," Mike admitted.

"School?" Jane asked.

"Yeah. Do they send my grades to you, like they did in high school?"

"Either that or you'll send them to me. Won't you?"

He nodded. "You're not gonna like them much. All

60

C's, unless some instructors take pity on me."

"Oh, Mike," Jane said, knowing she sounded terribly disappointed in spite of her resolve to be supportive. "You were a straight-A student in high school."

"Yeah, but I knew why I was doing it. I was working at getting A's so I could get into college and now I'm there and don't know why. See what I mean?"

"Not exactly."

"I don't know what's next . . . why I'm doing this . . . where I'm headed."

"But you know wherever you're headed you need a college degree to get there."

"Sure. But in what? One of my nerdy roommates knows he wants to be an accountant so he's taking all these math and business courses besides the basic stuff and he's acing everything. Mom, he doesn't know the difference between a fork and a spoon, but he knows what he wants to be. Another one is taking all this science stuff and likes it so much he wants to talk about it all the time. Genes and DNA and that. I'm just taking all this dumb college freshman stuff. English, algebra, earth science. I've already aced those in high school."

"And now you're getting C's in the same things? They're that much harder?"

"No, the courses aren't hard at all. In fact, some are a lot easier than high school. It's just 'cause they're so boring. I want to be really, really interested in something. I want to be like John, spouting about double helixes because I think they're so neat I can't keep it to myself."

"But Mike, you're interested in—and knowledge-able about—a lot of things."

"Uh-huh. Too many. I'm pretty good at sports, but I don't have dreams about making touchdowns. I can play a couple instruments, but I'm not good enough to make it my life's work. I know all the grammar rules and have big chunks of *Macbeth* memorized, but you can't make a living with that stuff. Besides, I don't want to."

Jane dumped the broccoli flowerettes into a bowl and started peeling the stalks and cutting them into slices. "Okay, I'm getting the picture. Yesterday I was asking Shelley for advice and she said she'd like to be the wise woman and give it to me, but had none. I feel sort of the same way. But I do have a few suggestions."

"Yeah?"

"First, get the grades in the dumb courses up."

"Yeah, I know that. I will. Piece of cake, really."

"Second, get it out of your head that you have to decide right now what you're going to be for the rest of your life. You've got at least two years before you have to even pick a major—and even then you can change it. Third, go get the college catalog. I saw a copy in your room when I was cleaning it up after Thanksgiving."

"Why the catalog?"

"Because I want you to go through it and mark the

weirdest courses you can find and take at least two of them every semester. If they're upper level and you can't actually enroll for credit, at least you can audit them. It doesn't matter if your first two years of required courses take two and a half or three years. There's enough money in the trust I set up for you with your dad's life insurance money to spring for an extra year if you want."

Mike went upstairs with what Jane imagined was a little bit of a spring in his step. He returned to the kitchen with the catalog open. He was laughing to himself.

"Here's a good one. 'The History of Armor: From Leather to Kevlar.' "

"Sign up for it," Jane said, dumping the broccoli stems in the pot of water that was now at the boil.

"Omigawd!" Mike exclaimed. "How about this one: 'Mortuary Science: Chemistry, Cosmetics, and Counseling.' I can't believe it."

"I sure hope that's not something you'd take and want to blab about at home. Although it would probably go over great in a dorm."

Mike found courses in gender bias in the military, an art class called "Color and Psychology," a history class titled "Catherine the Great: Was She?", a course in flower arranging ("Flower arranging?" Jane exclaimed. "Are there parents actually paying for their kids to take that?"), and several revolting-sounding premed courses.

"Mom, you're great!" Mike finally said. "Even if I

don't take any of this stuff, you've sure made me feel a lot better." He bounced off to his room, still flipping through the course catalog.

Am I great? Jane wondered. *No, probably not.*

But she was doing her best and if her best was just making her son feel better about himself, that wasn't too shabby an accomplishment. And who could tell— it might turn out that Mike would actually want to be a mortician, or an armor-maker.

She tossed the broccoli flowerettes into the steamer sitting over the boiling stems and started the white sauce.

Seven

Jane went on checking off items on her oh-so-efficient list. By three o'clock she was feeling that hosting the caroling party was no big deal and with a little organizational effort, she could entertain more often. Possibly quite spectacularly.

She managed to put out of her mind the many other times she'd believed herself to be highly organized only to discover that she'd omitted some vital consideration. Once, with a houseful of people, several of whom had occasion to use the bathroom, she'd run out of toilet paper. Another time she prepared to start the coffee for a party as the first guest arrived and realized the coffee can contained only a few disgusting crumbs. On both these occasions Shelley had bailed her out.

But this time, she truly believed she was prepared for anything that could happen.

She was wrong.

At quarter after three, Mel called. "I've just picked my mom up from the airport and she's dying to meet you," he said. "Is this a good time?"

Jane had never really wanted to meet Mel's mother. He always spoke of her very fondly and Jane could find no specific fault with what she'd heard about Addie VanDyne. It just amounted to a vague uneasiness.

But she said, "It's a perfect time. I don't have to put the potato casseroles in until—" She consulted her list. "—five-fifteen."

This didn't make much sense to Mel, but he didn't question her. "I think we may have a slight problem," he said. "I'll tell you about it when we get there."

In her current cocky mood, the concept of a slight problem didn't trouble Jane. She was Woman, she could cope. Little problems were mere trivialities. She quickly threw together a big green salad. This was marked as a four o'clock job, but it probably wouldn't wilt too badly if done a bit early. She glanced out the window while tearing lettuce and noticed that it had begun to snow again. Big, fluffy white flakes that were quickly covering the ground, but melting on the street. If it didn't get a lot colder and glaze over, the snow would be nice, adding a very traditional Christmas touch to the party.

She refreshed her hair and makeup, changed into a

fresh blouse and slacks because she'd inexplicably gotten tomato juice and seeds all over herself. *They ought to be here any minute,* she thought as she sat down in the living room to wait, idly flipping through a holiday crafts magazine while she tried to remember what she knew about Mel's family and why she had a sense that she and Addie weren't going to be on exactly the same wavelength. Mel didn't talk about his relations very often. His father had died young and his mother, if Jane was remembering right, had started an escort service in Atlanta. Not *that* kind of escort service, he'd hastily explained. A real one, driving visiting celebrities and rich business types around town. Ted Turner's television network had been God's gift to her. She invested in a limo and did the driving herself at first, then as she became more successful, she purchased more cars and hired drivers. She had eventually expanded the service to a number of Southern cities, franchising the business and traveling frequently to keep a close eye on the efficiency, courtesy, and driving skills of the drivers and the manner in which the home offices were run.

An admirable woman, Jane had thought. But now that she was about to meet Mel's mother, she had a few uncomfortable second thoughts. Jane herself had been widowed with young children and hadn't done anything nearly so impressive or financially aggressive. Thanks to life and mortgage insurance, and her own and her late husband's investment in his family's small chain of pharmacies, the profit from which hadn't died with him, she'd been able to be a stay-at-home, full-time mother. She had no regrets. Raising her children was a job that was both challenging and important to her and she felt she'd done it fairly well so far.

And her contribution to the outside world was substantial as well. She volunteered for a great many worthwhile endeavors. Once a week she drove a group of blind children to their special school that had no bus service. She served, albeit unwillingly, on the PTA board and had often allowed herself to be dragooned into being a room mother. She worked for her church and several charities and had served on the fundraising committees for a number of civic groups. But all of that might well appear pretty inconsequential to a woman who had started a highly successful business from scratch.

She heard Mel's red MG pull into the driveway—she *had* to get that pothole at the end of it fixed soon or his little car would disappear into it someday. She had visions of firemen lowering rope ladders into the hole. She opened the front door to greet them.

The snow was getting heavier and Mel introduced his mother while they crowded into the house, shaking snowflakes from hair and shoulders. "Mom, this is Jane Jeffry. Jane, my mother, Addie VanDyne."

Jane was stunned. The woman hardly looked more than a couple years older than Jane herself. She had masses of curly dark hair; a valentine-shaped face without a single wrinkle that Jane could see; small, sparkling white teeth and big china-blue eyes. She was—well, there was no other word—cute, in a very expensive, sophisticated way. She wore a black cashmere coat, black patent boots, and the same elegant black gloves Jane had wanted to get Shelley for Christmas but simply couldn't afford. As Addie Van-Dyne shed her coat, she revealed a slubbed silk princess-line suit that precisely matched her eyes and did wonders for her perfect figure. She even had a dimple, just like Mel's, which enhanced the impression that she might just be a slightly older sister instead of his mother.

Jane wanted to run away and burn her own khaki slacks and plaid shirt.

She hung up their coats and indicated they were to make themselves comfortable in the living room. As she closed the closet door, she noticed there was an unfamiliar suitcase sitting in the hall. Mel must have brought it in. Dear God, Addie VanDyne hadn't brought them presents, had she? This possibility had never crossed Jane's mind. She'd prepared for the visit with a nice bottle of perfume and an elegant little atomizer in an Erte-like design which was wrapped in fancy red foil for Mel's mother, but that was all.

Jane had coffee and tea ready to put into the antique, but somewhat shabby, slightly dented silver service that had been a wedding present from her grandmother, and she'd arranged a plate of cookies—good ones, not the deformed elves. She filled the tray and took it into the living room.

"I thought you might like a little snack after your trip, Mrs. VanDyne. We're having quite a big dinner later."

She expected Mel's mom to insist on being called Addie, but instead she said, "How thoughtful, Mrs. Jeffry." Was there a little emphasis on the "Mrs." or did Jane only imagine it?

Jane asked a few inane questions about Mrs. VanDyne's flight to which she got pleasant, innocuous replies. Mel tried to help. "Mom, tell Jane about the man with the dog in a carrier," he said rather desperately.

Mrs. VanDyne waved this away. "It wasn't that interesting, dear." She glanced around the room. "What a very nice little house you have, Mrs. Jeffry. I suppose these holiday decorations have some family significance."

In other words, they look like shit but must mean something to me, otherwise I wouldn't let them see the light of day, Jane thought. *No, don't get off on the wrong foot,* she warned herself.

She nodded and turned to Mel. "You mentioned a little problem on the phone?" she asked meaningfully.

"My furnace has gone out and it's pretty arctic in my apartment," he said. "Mom had a bout of pneumonia last year and really can't take the cold . . ."

Jane saw what was coming and mentally crossed her fingers that she was wrong.

69

"I wondered if maybe she could camp out here with you until it's fixed," he said.

Jane realized she should have tried serious prayer instead of superstition.

"Mel, dear," Mrs. VanDyne said, "I told you I'd be happy to stay in a hotel."

"Mom, you're always complaining about how much you hate staying in hotels, since you have to do it so much of the time. Jane's got a guest room and it would only be for one night. I'm sure Jane wouldn't mind. And it would give you two a chance to get to know each other better."

He was smiling as if this were a great idea they'd both welcome.

Jane was running through several appealing choices of how to kill him. What nerve, dumping his mother on her without warning and right in front of the woman. And he looked so damned cheerful, as if he really believed what he was saying. And the thing was, he probably did.

"I'd be glad to have you stay here," Jane said, giving Mel an "I'll Get Even with You If It Takes the Rest of My Life" look.

"Oh, I couldn't impose on you."

In that case, why had she let Mel bring her suitcase in, Jane wondered. "It wouldn't be the slightest imposition . . . Addie." If the woman was going to stay here, she was going to be called by her first name, Jane decided.

"Well, thank you . . . Jane. If you're quite sure?"

Mel beamed. Jane wanted to smack him. Thank goodness she'd given the guest room, which was hardly more than a good-sized closet and usually full of craft junk, a thorough cleaning. Or maybe not. Addie wouldn't have been quite so inclined to stay if she'd had to wrestle with measuring tapes, an ironing board, quilting pins, and the sewing machine to get to the bed. And sharing a bathroom with all three kids wasn't going to be a lot of fun for her either.

Maybe I'm misjudging her, Jane thought, trying to be both fair and noble. *Maybe Mel's right and we'll get to be friends by being thrown together this way.* Probably not, but anything was possible.

"Mel, if you want to take Addie and her suitcase upstairs, I need to make a quick phone call and get some things into the oven."

As they went up the stairs, Jane raced for the phone and dialed Shelley. "Disaster," she said softly when Shelley answered. "Mel's dumped his mother on me. To stay at my house until his furnace is fixed!"

"He *didn't!*" Shelley exclaimed.

"I can't have her underfoot while I'm throwing this dinner together. Please come divert her for a little while."

"Give me five minutes to stuff the hams into the oven and I'll be there."

Jane had just hung up the phone when Mel came into the kitchen. "Mom's changing her clothes. I've got to go back to my apartment and wait for the furnace people," he said. "I hope you don't mind keeping Mom overnight, Janey."

"I wouldn't have minded a private warning," Jane said frankly. "I don't really have much free time to entertain her."

"Oh, she won't need entertaining. She's really self-sufficient. And she's a great cook. Maybe she can help you with dinner."

"I don't *need* help, Mel. I'm a good cook, too."

"I know you are." He paused, jingling his car keys. "Janey, you're not pissed off, are you?"

"Aren't I?" Jane asked, heading for the garage to bring in the scalloped potato casseroles.

When she came back into the kitchen, he was looking contrite. "I'm sorry. I got rattled and didn't think. I should have asked you first, but I didn't know I'd need to ask at all until we got to my apartment and it was freezing cold. She really did have a bad time with the pneumonia last year and—"

"I know, Mel." She remembered when he went to visit his ailing mother. Jane had pictured Addie Van-Dyne as a little old lady with white hair and a frail, almost-ready-for-the-nursing-home constitution. That had obviously been a stupid assumption. Jane's own mother was older than Mel's and she was fit and sleek as a racehorse.

"Listen, Janey. I'll take her to a hotel. I'll tell her . . . something."

"You'd have to tell a whopping great lie that she'd know was one," Jane said, sliding the casserole into the oven—which she now realized she'd forgotten to preheat. "I'm not going to throw your mother out. It's okay. It's a done deal. And, as you say, it's just for one night."

"You really don't want her here, do you? You don't like her?"

He sounded so astonished at the very concept that Jane could think of nothing to say except, "I'm sure I'll like her a lot, Mel. We don't even know each other yet. Now, get out of my way. I have a ton of stuff to do before the party. You *are* coming, aren't you?"

"The minute the furnace repair person leaves," he said, looking cheerful again.

Jane heard Addie coming down the stairs a few minutes after Mel left. Jane had assumed that Addie had changed into more comfortable sitting-around-the-house clothing although it was too much to hope she'd opt for a sweatsuit.

Addie swished into the kitchen wearing a cherry red outfit that Jane could only think of as "lounging pajamas." There was a lovely self-stripe to the fabric, which draped beautifully, and Addie had added a necklace and earrings of silver and Christmas tree–green stones that Jane feared were real emeralds.

"How can I help, Jane dear?"

"You could start by loaning me your wardrobe," Jane said.

"What?"

"Just a joke," Jane said.

73

Eight

Shelley came to her rescue in fine form, engaging Addie in light, impersonal conversation so that Jane could finish dinner preparations. Every now and then Shelley would toss Jane a question. An easy one, like "Do you need any help?" or "How's it going?" To which Jane could reply brightly, "Not a bit," or "It's coming right along on schedule."

As six o'clock approached, the time the carolers were to assemble, several neighbors dropped in with contributions. Sharon Wilhite made a couple of trips, bringing four very expensive-looking wine bottles and a box full of plastic wineglasses. "Hope you don't mind them being plastic," Sharon said.

"Is there anyone on earth with thirty real ones sitting around?" Jane asked. "Plastic is great."

"I hear Lance King's invited to the party," Sharon said.

"And he's been uninvited," Jane said bluntly. "Sorry, maybe you're a fan of his."

"Fan? No way. He was born obnoxious. I often wonder . . . oh, well, never mind."

This was the sort of conversational gambit Jane would normally have pursued avidly, but was too busy at the moment. She'd ask Sharon about it later. If she could remember.

Julie Newton brought snack mix and, to Jane's surprise, had the native wit to bring along little matched bowls the shape of Christmas trees to set around the house on various flat surfaces. Little Pet Dwyer turned up with a pan of fudge she'd made herself. It looked like a big mud pie with green sprinkles, but the women all complimented her skills effusively.

"Are you and your dad singing with the group before you come here for dinner?" Jane asked.

"No, Daddy has to work at home tonight. But he said I could come if someone would walk me home by eight-thirty. He's putting together a web page that has a lot of graphics to load."

"I'm sure Todd will be happy to walk you home, Pet," Jane told her. "Be sure your father knows he's welcome to drop by if he gets a chance to take a break. Lots of good food here."

"Thank you, Mrs. Jeffry," Pet said in such a formal tone that it sounded like a verbal curtsy.

As soon as she'd gone, Todd came in with his friend Elliott and they had to be severely reprimanded to stay out of the fudge and to quit making fun of the way it looked. Katie brought her friend Jenny to the house as well. Jenny's mother had sent chips and dip with them which had suffered only a few depredations along the way.

Suzie Williams showed up at the same time with four bags of ice and a half-set Jell-O salad. "Sorry, it was the best I could do. Inventory week. Want me to put the ice in your basement freezer?"

Mike had spontaneously decided to make one last

vacuum-cleaner run through the downstairs rooms and they were all having to shout over the noise. Jane glanced at Addie, who was looking befuddled at the Grand Central Station atmosphere.

Addie caught the look and asked, "Is it always like this around here?"

"Not always," Jane said, trying to sound very calm and competent. "Sometimes it's quiet. Sometimes it's worse. Remember slumber parties?"

"My girls never had them," Addie said. "I was gone too much of the time in the evenings when they were the slumber party age. My sister helped me take care of them. I didn't feel I could burden her with that."

This gave Shelley another conversational gambit to pursue and she took off after it like a greyhound. Jane could tell by Shelley's too-polite tone and faintly brittle smile that she wasn't really taking to Addie VanDyne. She also knew full well that Shelley would know better than to let Addie know how she felt.

Jane set a big pasta pot full of seasoned apple cider on the stove and checked her list once more. Done. She was done! All that remained was to set everything out on the table when the gang of singers got close to her house.

Suzie emerged from the basement. "Omigawd!" Jane exclaimed. "I forgot you were down there, Suzie. You scared me to death!"

"Your son and his friend are playing a blood-and-guts game on your computer. I hung around for a while to watch. Cool stuff. Gotta go put on my thermal undies and sing my brains out." She looked at Addie, to whom she'd been introduced on her way to the basement. "You're not going out in that outfit, are you?"

Addie obviously didn't know whether to be offended or amused. "No, I'm staying inside. I can hold the fort here if you want to go along, Jane."

"I'm just going to watch from the front porch," Jane said. "I've had too long a day to wade through the snow."

"How does this work?" Addie asked. "If everybody's singing, who's being sung to?"

Shelley answered. "The couple at the far end of the street start by going next door. Then the people in that house can join them to go to the next. There are a number of neighbors, some of the older ones in particular, who don't want to go out in the cold. And there are a few like Jane who couldn't carry a tune if it had handles attached."

"Cruel, Shelley," Jane said with a laugh. "True, but cruel."

Shelley and Suzie left together, but Shelley was back a moment later, looking grim. "Jane, you're not going to like this," she said. "But there's a television camera crew set up at the end of the block."

As Jane had feared, Lance King's gracious bowing out had been a sham. For reasons of his own, he'd gotten his teeth into the neighborhood party and was determined to do his newscast from the site.

"But why?" Jane wondered aloud to Shelley. "His speciality is rabid exposés. How could he have whipped one up so fast and who's his intended victim?"

"I have no idea. But there might be a bright side," Shelley said. "I never watch the channel he's on anymore because he's so nasty it makes my blood boil to even see him. Maybe he's mellowed."

"Or maybe the station manager had forced him to do some positive stories. Unlikely, but possible," Jane said.

"Who is this person you're talking about?" Addie put in. Jane had forgotten that Addie was there.

"A local rabble-rouser television person. Lance King."

"Lance King!" Addie exclaimed.

"You know about him?" Jane asked, surprised that his notoriety reached as far as Atlanta.

"I've seen him on television when I visited Mel. Thoroughly distasteful man. And he's out there filming the caroling? He's not coming to your house with them, is he?"

She seemed overly alarmed by this, considering how little she knew about Lance King, Jane thought. "Unfortunately, I imagine that's what he has in mind."

"So, what are you going to do, Jane?" Shelley asked.

"I don't know. If I let him in, he'll ruin the party. If I keep him out, he'll make a scene and still ruin the party. And probably find a way to ruin me as well."

They heard the singing start and Shelley said, "I'm

going to join them. Send one of your kids over for the hams. The kitchen door's unlocked."

Jane would have liked to indulge herself in a good cry in the bathroom, but even that was denied her. The phone rang and it was Mel. "I'll be over in a couple minutes, Janey. The furnace fixer didn't show up and I'm going to have to start over tomorrow with another company, I guess."

"Okay," she said between gritted teeth.

She sent Todd and Elliott for the hams and made Katie go along to find and identify the pineapple-mustard sauce. "As soon as you've got everything, you can go join the rest of the singers."

She bundled herself up and went to observe and listen from the front porch. A couple deep, cold breaths helped her calm down slightly and the sound of the neighbors' voices raised in a rousing version of "Jingle Bells" didn't hurt. She reminded herself of her long-standing party philosophy, which was that it's pointless to have a party if you're not going to enjoy it yourself. The planning and preparation might be tough, but the panic to get ready had to stop the moment the first guest stepped through the door.

"I can do this," she said to herself. "And Lance King can't wreck it." She watched as a television cameraman posed a small collection of singers in front of an especially pretty house. A man in a Santa suit—King himself—was standing in the middle of the arrangement.

As she stood, watching and listening to the ever-

growing group going from house to house, one of the
television people broke away from the group and
walked briskly down the street to Jane's house. The
woman approaching her was young, very tall, and had
a mop of curly maroon-red hair escaping her stocking
cap. She walked leaning forward, hands plunged into
the pockets of a pea jacket and a clipboard under one
arm. "Are you Mrs. Jeffry?" she said. "I'm Ginger
Wrightman, Mr. King's assistant. I need to take a look
at the house layout and figure out where to set up the
lights and camera."

"Mr. King wasn't invited to my house," Jane said.
"Or, he was, but without my permission."

Ginger said, "Oh, I didn't know. I'm so sorry.
But—"

"But I don't dare lock him out," Jane finished. "I'm
aware of that. Come on in, Ginger."

As Ginger shed her cap and coat, she apologized
again. "I'm just an employee, Mrs. Jeffry. I don't
know how much longer I can take it, either. I'm just
too damned nice for this job."

Jane studied Ginger. She wasn't pretty by any means.
Her face was too elongated, her nose and teeth too big,
her eyes too close together and her hair was dead
awful. But there was something terribly vulnerable
about this plain young woman's honesty that charmed
Jane. "I understand. Make yourself at home."

Jane went back out on the porch. When she judged
the carolers were close enough to arrive at her home
in another ten minutes, she went inside.

Addie pitched in and helped set the food out, annoying Jane enormously by changing where Jane had chosen to put the dishes. "There," Addie exclaimed. "That looks much better with the hams farther apart, doesn't it?"

"I guess so," Jane said wearily, wishing she could shove Addie into a closet for just long enough to get the table set up the way she'd intended. As soon as everyone had been through the line once, Jane was going to put the desserts out on the kitchen table and counter. Mel had better be there by then to keep his mother out of her hair.

Ginger found Jane in the kitchen. "I think we can set up in a way that won't completely destroy your party. Lance will be doing a short commercial feed live at eight. Just a fifteen-second bit. Then later he'll open the news live with a two-minute piece. Of course, we can pray there's real news by then that'll take precedence."

"A nice plane wreck or a bomb going off somewhere?" Jane said.

Ginger grinned. "Something like that. Think you could arrange it?"

People started coming in the front door, shaking snow off their clothes, piling coats, hats, and mittens on the stairs, the banister, and the coat-rack Jane had borrowed from Shelley. Pet was among the first to arrive, and being a model child, she assigned herself the job of making sure the hats and gloves stayed with the right coats.

"I'm hiring that child the next time I put on a do," Jane said as Shelley came inside.

"It's starting to rain," Shelley said. "All the snow will have melted by morning."

Jane looked at her with amazement. "Are you actually making light meaningless chitchat to take my mind off that horrible man who's going to invade my house any second?"

Shelley grinned. "I guess I am. Listen, Jane, you have to think about this like I do about getting a Pap test. No matter how awful it's going to be, in X number of hours it's going to be over."

"Well, X number of hours can't pass fast enough for me," Jane said grimly.

The party got off to a rousing start, everybody being glad to get out of the cold and eat themselves silly. But when Lance King finally rejoined the group, with his cameraman, lighting people, and equipment, the crowd in Jane's house grew significantly quieter and more subdued. Nobody, it seemed, wanted to attract his attention except a couple malcontents who fell on him with suggestions for individuals they personally wanted skewered.

Jane lurked at the kitchen door, watching Lance move through the room like a bad smell. Nobody actually recoiled, hand over nose, but they looked away, got very interested in minute items on their plates, or struck up quietly animated conversations with each other.

Lance didn't seem to care. He strolled about the

room as if he were a rock star and the rest were adoring fans. He carried a bag, which Jane assumed was a laptop computer, and carelessly banged it into several pieces of furniture. His Santa suit was open at the neck and he'd discarded his false beard somewhere. Probably in the middle of the dining room table where it could remain a revolting reminder of his presence, Jane thought nastily.

"Ho! Ho! Ho!" he suddenly bellowed. There was a soft clatter of plastic utensils as several startled partygoers lost their grips on forks and spoons. "This looks more like a wake than a holiday party. Ah, life in the suburbs. Ever exciting."

He gazed around for a moment, then noticed Jane at the kitchen door. He called across the room, "You must be Mrs. Jeffry. Thanks for inviting us to your happy little home." He flung himself into Jane's favorite chair, the squashy, overstuffed one that was so comfortable that she considered sitting in it as going back to the womb. It was where she sat to watch television, to play with her laptop, to do double-crostics. Her chair had been violated.

"I didn't," Jane muttered.

"What was that? Speak up, honey."

Jane balled her fists as she felt a flush flood her face and she turned away. She headed for the guest bathroom in the little hall leading to the garage, considering the possibility that she could just keep going. Get in the car, drive away, and come back later. Instead, she shut herself in the bathroom for a few quiet minutes of rage. But training eventually overcame emotions. Jane's father was in the State Department and she'd grown up all over the world. And she'd been told, practically from birth, that the host or hostess must be polite to guests—no matter what. No running away or hiding in bathrooms. As a child and teenager, she'd attended various dinners her parents gave that included sheep's eyeballs, petrified codfish, and eating on the floor of a tent with the sound of wild animals just outside. Lance King was only marginally more revolting than any of those.

She emerged and found herself face-to-face with Mel.

"I've been looking all over for you, Janey," he said. "What's wrong? You look upset."

"Probably because I am."

"It's not my mother, is it?" he asked, looking suddenly wary.

Jane managed to laugh. "No." She almost added, *"Not this time,"* but resisted the temptation. "It's that jerk Lance King."

"He's here?"

"Here? Of course. How could you have missed him?"

Mel put his arm around her and walked her slowly back through the kitchen. Jane noticed that the volume of the party had gone back up to normal. "He must have left. Thank goodness. Maybe Ginger arranged for that airplane crash after all."

By the time she finished explaining who Ginger was and what she meant, Jane felt considerably better. "Thanks for listening," she said, leaning her head against his shoulder. "I'm going to go enjoy my own party."

Jane, the diplomat's daughter, made her rounds, making sure she welcomed everyone individually and cordially. At ten minutes to eight, Lance King reappeared with his television makeup and the fake beard back in place. Ginger helped shuffle people out of the way of the electrical cords and lighting stands and at one minute to eight, held up one hand and stared at her watch.

When her hand dropped, Lance King smiled broadly and looked into the camera with a lizard-like smile. "A neighborhood block party in celebration of the holidays. What could be more fun? More innocent? Nice people and good food. But is there a dark underbelly to this happy, if not to say smug, suburban life? Tune in to the late news and find out."

The television lighting went off and there was a moment of dead silence. Lance King pulled off his beard, looked around the room, and strode out of the house, laughing.

Nine

There was a long, frigid moment of silence as Lance King walked out the front door, slamming the door behind himself.

Then Billy Joe Johnson, who had mistakenly assumed this was a costume party and was dressed as a rotund snowman, said, "Who is that guy and why's he being so darned nasty?"

Fairy Princess Tiffany said, "He must be a television person. What with the cameras and all. Wonder if we'll all be on the news." She apparently had paid no attention at all to the content of his broadcast.

Somebody muttered, "The bastard." Jane thought the remark came from one of Lance's own crew, but couldn't be sure.

Ginger, her long face flushed and blotchy, grabbed Jane's arm. "I'm so sorry. And if it helps any—which I know it won't—I'm unemployed as of this moment. Voluntarily!"

"What peculiar behavior," a woman from the mock Tudor house at the far end of the block said, setting her plate on an end table and rising. "I'm certainly not planning to be here when he returns to make another distasteful display. Jane, where's my coat?"

A half dozen or so of the guests departed in a mob. None of them looked frightened especially, only disgusted. Jane helped find coats and saw them off with broken apologies, trying to make everyone understand that she had most assuredly not invited Lance King to the party. She was even good-hearted enough to refrain from mentioning that this was all Julie Newton's fault.

As she watched them leave, she said, "Mel, can I get a police officer at the door to keep him from coming back into my house?"

"Janey, calm down."

Her eyes filled with tears of fury and frustration. "I'll hire a private security guard then. I wonder how you find one on short notice."

She felt something tugging her sleeve. "Mrs. Jeffry," Pet said, "I should go home soon."

Jane put her hand on Pet's thin little shoulder. "Yes, dear." She spotted Todd bounding up the stairs. "Todd, put on your coat and boots. Pet needs to be walked home."

"Mom! It's just down the block a couple hous—"

"Todd," Jane said in a low, menacing tone that made his eyes widen.

"Oh . . . okay. Right away."

Jane left Mel to see the children off and watch for Todd's return while she went back to the kitchen to look for a phone book. She was quite serious about hiring someone to keep Lance away. She'd toss his television equipment out in the front yard so she couldn't be accused of stealing anything from him.

She heard muffled sobbing and followed the sound to the little bathroom next to the kitchen. "Julie? Is that you? Come out here right now and let me beat you about the head," Jane said firmly.

The door opened a crack and Julie peered out with one eye. "Oh, Jane—" she wailed, suddenly opening the door and flinging herself into Jane's arms. "I'm so, so sorry. He's so horrible. I had no idea. What can I do? How can I ever, ever make this up to you?"

"By sitting down with the phone book right here and hiring a security firm to get over here right now and keep him from coming back into my house," Jane said, disentangling herself from Julie's embrace. "And *you're* paying for it."

"Oh, yes. Of course. Thank you. I'll do that," Julie babbled between sniffles and hiccups.

"There's a phone and phone book upstairs in my bedroom."

Julie hurried to do as she was told.

Shelley came into the kitchen a second later. "Thank God you're here, Jane. I've been looking for you. I was afraid you were out looking for him with an Uzi."

"None of my Uzis are oiled. Or primed. Whatever. I don't really know what an Uzi is, come to think of it. But right now I wouldn't mind acquiring one."

Mel entered the room as she was speaking. "Jane, that's not really funny."

"Mel, *none* of this is funny!"

He knew when the river of affection was running at full flood the wrong way. "No, it's not. I'm sorry."

She sighed. It wasn't his fault. "Is Todd back?"

Mel nodded. "Yes, all your chicks are home and safe

88

in spite of all the traffic. The street looks like there's a parade going on with all the gawkers at the Johnsons' house."

She smiled weakly. "And I guess everybody else has left, huh? Think of the leftovers we'll have. I hadn't even put the desserts out yet."

"No," Mel said. "You've still got a mob out there."

"You're kidding!" Jane edged around him and looked into the living room. He was right. "Why don't they go home while the getting's good?"

Shelley spoke up. "Some of them still think it's a joke. The rest are ghouls. By the way, that woman who lives next door to Suzie asked me what agency you used to hire the Johnsons. She thought they were actors pretending to be hillbillies."

Suddenly Jane's accumulated tension dropped away. She started laughing. There was an edge of hysteria to it. "No, Shelley, don't get that look," she said between giggles. "And don't get any ideas about slapping me to my senses. I'm okay. It's just that—"

She went off again.

Billy Joe swaggered in from the living room, bumping a bowl of pretzels off an occasional table with his oversized snowman butt. "Wondered where's you got to, Jane. Oops, sorry." He tried to lean over to pick up the pretzels, but with the fat costume, he couldn't reach the floor.

Jane rushed over and pulled him back upright. "Never mind, I'll just sweep them under the table for now."

"What are you laughing about?" he said.

"Nothing at all. I'm just happy you're here. That's all."

Billy Joe looked pleased and deeply embarrassed. "Shucks," he mumbled.

An hour later, Jane was nearly back to normal. Ginger had forced the cameraman and the rest of the crew and equipment outdoors. The crew had left the electrical cords plugged into an outside socket and gone off in their van to have coffee and keep warm at a nearby convenience store.

Julie had struck out on security guards, but Jane was resolved to simply lock the doors when Lance returned. It was probably just as well that she hadn't been able to surround her house with armed guards. Imagine what Lance could have made of that. He could have yapped about it on the nightly news for weeks.

Jane could just imagine the headline: "Suburban housewife barricades house against seeker of truth—what dirty secret is she hiding?" That was Lance's style.

Most of the guests had professed the intention of leaving well before the newscast and kept glancing at their watches. But they were determined not to waste a good party and seemed to be thoroughly enjoying the exchange of neighborhood gossip. A couple of the men—and Suzie, naturally—gravitated to the basement where they fooled around with Jane's computer and talked RAM, ROM, and modem speeds. Jane's dog Willard had been confined to the basement for the evening and was thrilled to have company. Her cats Max and Meow, who didn't like strangers in *their* house, had retreated indignantly to the laundry room.

A clump of women gathered in the kitchen, picking at the remaining desserts and talking about diets, their jobs, shopping, and, mostly, the atrocities of having the kids home all day for two weeks. One complained bitterly about the Johnsons' house attracting so much traffic to the block. (*The Concerned Citizen, no doubt,* Jane thought.) A handful of people who were devotees of *It's a Wonderful Life* settled in the living room to watch it for the sixty-seventh time on television. One of the men kept asking if he couldn't just see if there was a sports channel during a commercial and was hooted down. If it hadn't been for the threat of Lance King's return hanging over her, Jane would have judged it a perfect party.

Julie Newton had finally finished crying and apologizing and was talking to anybody who would listen about the progress of her new kitchen. Addie had made friends with a woman who was a regional book rep and they were having a good jaw about the horrors of getting out-of-town authors around to the bookstores. "She would never take a flight after seven in the evening or before ten in the morning, had to have a bottle of chilled champagne in the car at all times, and carried more luggage than Hannibal crossing the Alps," Jane overheard Addie telling the other woman.

Jane's neighbor nodded sagely. "When we sent her out on tour, she insisted on dragging along her hairdresser, too."

Shelley and Jane crossed paths as Jane headed upstairs for potty break and Shelley came down the steps from the same errand. "It's turned into a decent party after all, hasn't it?" Shelley said.

"It has," Jane said. "A credit to my hostessing skills."

"You *are* a good party-giver, Jane. Better than I am," Shelley said.

Jane laughed. "That's because I let people do what they want. You tell them where to sit and what they should talk about."

"I do not! I merely make helpful suggestions. And try to put people together who have common interests."

"Uh-huh. Like that voter registration meeting you had at your house and you made that rabid prochoice woman and the Operation Rescue guy sit together?"

"I've already admitted that was a mistake, Jane," Shelley said haughtily. "You don't need to keep harping on it. Still, I think they could have had an enlightening exchange of views if they'd only stopped screaming at each other."

"Maybe, but when they got to the drink-flinging stage, it was too late."

Jane went on upstairs and when she came back down, Julie was in the front hall in her hat and coat.

"My baby-sitter has to leave at nine-thirty. I'm afraid I've got to go."

Jane didn't believe the baby-sitter story for a second. Julie was just trying to escape being on the scene when Lance came back and discovered he was locked out. But that was okay. Jane couldn't bear another round of hysterical apologizing.

"Bundle up, then. It's nasty outside," Jane said. "May I keep your little snack dishes for the cookie party tomorrow afternoon?"

"Oh, please do," Julie said as Jane opened the front door for her. "I have more of the snack mix, too. I'll come early and refill the dishes."

Julie stepped out the door and started down the steps. As she reached the bottom she turned, presumably for one last repentant remark, but in doing so, her glance went over the Johnsons' front yard.

She stopped. Stared.

Her eyes opened very wide and then she screamed.

Jane lurched out onto the porch. Julie was pointing at the Johnsons' house. At first Jane couldn't imagine what was so frightening. It wasn't as if Julie hadn't seen the hideous decorations before. Then Jane's attention, like Julie's, focused on the sleigh and reindeer in the front, just outside the Johnsons' living room windows.

One of the lead reindeers had collapsed. And there was something red lying across its plaster head.

A body. In a Santa suit.

Jane stepped back inside the door where others were

already gathering to see what Julie was screaming about and shouted, *"MEL!"*

Ten

"I can only stay a minute, but I wanted to let you know what little we know so far. King slid off the Johnsons' roof," Mel said several hours later. "The skid marks are still there, but they're melting fast. The plaster reindeer had some sort of metal spike that came out of its head to hold the antlers in place. One of them got him in the heart."

There was a collective shudder. Most of the guests were long gone, after having stood around in Jane's front yard for a long time watching the police, ambulance, and plain-clothes people work. Jane and Shelley sat on the sofa next to each other. Mike sat on the arm on Jane's side in a vaguely protective manner. Addie VanDyne had gone to bed, as had Todd and Katie. Ginger had stayed and had arranged her long, gangly self on the floor by the fire like a folding carpenter's ruler. She said, "I'm sorry if this sounds ugly, but I'm sure glad I didn't call the station manager to quit earlier this evening. I'll probably end up back in the secretarial pool, but it's better than working for Lance."

"What was he doing on the roof?" Jane asked Mel.

"I have no idea. Do you know, Ginger?" Mel replied.

"Snooping. Probably."

"Snooping on whom?" Mel asked.

Ginger shrugged. "He never confided in me. Or anybody else. His stories were as much of a surprise to the station as they were to the audience. Good thing he hit the reindeer. I mean, if he'd only gotten hurt, he'd have crucified the Johnsons in court. He knew all about insurance claims. One of his specialities."

"How'd he get up there?" Shelley asked. "It's not easy to get on a roof. Especially when you're in a Santa suit in the snow."

"Billy Joe had left a ladder out in the backyard when he finished his decorating," Mel said. "The back of the roof is a fairly shallow incline. Some owner must have had it raised to get more space upstairs."

Jane shook her head. "He was a wicked person, but he didn't seem stupid. The roof had all that slushy, slippery snow; even if it wasn't as steep as the front, it was still dangerous. What could he have wanted to watch badly enough to climb up there? And what if he hadn't seen it—whatever it was. Did he think he could lurk in the manger up there for days?"

Ginger spoke up again. "He was putting one of his gadgets up there, I'd guess. He had a slew of long-range listening devices and recorders and remote-control cameras. He even carried around night-vision binoculars in his car."

Shelley shivered. "What slime. And what a well-deserved accident."

There was a moment of quiet, then Jane said to Mel,

"I notice you're not commenting."

Mel cocked an eyebrow at her and said, carefully, "There is some evidence that it might not have been an accident."

"Come on," Ginger said. "Nobody commits suicide by flinging themselves off a roof onto a plaster reind— Oh, you mean—?"

"The usual question now," Mel said, "is: Did he have any enemies?"

"Have you got a notebook with lots of blank pages to fill? He had nothing but enemies," Jane said. "What kind of evidence are you talking about?"

"There appear to be two sets of footprints going up the back side of the roof. One only goes up and ends in a skid down the front. The other set goes up to the peak and then back down the back side to the ladder."

"Someone else was on the roof?" Shelley exclaimed. "Can't you get footprints? Or shoe prints, I guess."

"Too soggy," Mel said. "With the rain on top of the snow, they're just outlines. Can't even tell a size because of the snow melt."

"So someone pushed him off the roof," Jane said.

"That's jumping to conclusions," Mel said. "The two sets of prints were made at approximately the same time. Someone else could have been up there first and King was following him or her. Or somebody could have gone up after King fell."

"Why would anyone do that?" Mike asked.

Mel shrugged. "I'm just talking about physical possibilities. Not motives."

"But you still think somebody pushed him off the peak of the roof?" Jane asked.

"Without proof, I couldn't say, but if I were to guess, I'd suspect it was murder. And we have to treat it as such until we know. I've got to go. Ginger, do you know where he kept his files?"

"No files. He didn't want anyone to know what he was doing until he did it. I think he kept everything on his laptop."

"Which is where?" Mel asked.

Ginger pointed at the squashy armchair Jane was sitting in. "That looks like the case, next to the chair. Unless it's yours, Jane."

Jane peered over the arm of the chair. "No, mine's in a blue case. He did have this with him. He bashed into the coffee table with it and knocked a candle over."

Mel picked up the laptop. "Let me see you to your door, Shelley, and I'll have one of my people take Ginger to her car. Lock up carefully, Jane."

Mike helped Jane unload the dishwasher and put away the last of the leftover food and then he went to let the pets out of the basement. Max and Meow crept up the steps, wary that there might still be visitors in the house. When they were satisfied that there were no strangers present to try to pet them, they wound themselves sinuously around Jane's legs, demanding food.

"I'll run the vacuum in the morning," Jane said as

she opened a can of cat food. "I don't want to wake Addie with it this late at night. Will you keep Willard in your room tonight so he doesn't run loose and bark the house down?"

Mike nodded, petting Willard's big, square head. Glancing into the living room, he said, "Looks pretty good, considering. Mom, who do you think killed that guy?"

"I haven't any idea. It could have been anyone. He had a lot of enemies."

"But it has to be someone from around here, doesn't it?"

"I don't see why. With all the traffic on the street gawking at the Johnsons' house, anyone could have come into the neighborhood without being noticed."

"But how would they have known where to come?" Mike asked. "On that short television bit he just talked about 'a suburb.' He didn't say exactly where he was."

"Oh, maybe you're right," Jane said. "But someone could have seen the television van and guessed. Or followed him from the station."

That was just mother talk, she realized as she was getting ready for bed. The natural impulse to reassure her child—albeit an intelligent adult child—that his neighborhood was safe and he would come to no harm.

In truth, the neighborhood was less likely to come to harm with Lance King dead. It was an awful and cynical way to view the demise of a human being, but he had been a very dangerous man. A Life Wrecker. How did anyone get to be that way? What kind of background created someone who loved to be hated?

Jane had always felt it was an essential, bone-deep human trait to want to be liked. Or at least respected. Some people desperately wanted everybody to love them. That was one end of the scale. Most just needed the love of a few people—spouse, children, best friend—and respect from a larger number. But if you felt from early on in life that you couldn't acquire anyone's love, maybe power was the natural substitute.

Lance had accumulated more power than anyone needed or was good for them. Probably it was a case of getting a thrill out of seeing fear in people's faces. Fear could look like respect, Jane supposed.

She undressed and crawled into bed, shoving the cats aside. They'd left two lovely warm spots. She could hear muffled voices in the Johnsons' yard. The police, and Mel, were going to have a long night of it.

Mike was right, she thought sleepily. If the obvious conclusion—murder—was right, somebody they knew had probably committed it.

Jane was up early, having her coffee in front of the little kitchen counter television. She tuned to the station Lance King had worked for. When the local news came on, she was astonished to see Ginger doing a live feed. She'd tidied up her hair and was standing on the street in front of the Johnsons' house. "Lance King, a familiar and popular reporter for this station, died here last night," she said, not sounding the least nervous at her elevation from assistant/gofer to reporter. "In a freak accident, King fell from the roof of this home and suffered fatal injuries. The police are not saying if they've determined whether it was an accident or foul play. Further reports will be made on the noon news and this evening we'll have a report on Lance King's life and career. Back to you, Ann."

Ann and Charles, the morning anchors who could have passed for Barbie and Ken, looked suitably solemn for a few seconds, then Ann smiled and launched into a piece on local children's activities during the holidays that harried moms and dads could take the kids to. Jane turned off the television and went to the front window.

Ginger had divested herself of her microphone and was heading for Jane's front door. Jane opened it for her and invited her in. "I just saw you on the news," Jane said, leading the way back to the kitchen. "You looked great and sounded very polished." She got down a fresh cup and poured coffee for Ginger.

"I hope I didn't flub anything," Ginger said.

"Do you know anything more that you weren't saying?" Jane asked bluntly.

"No, not really. But I've been at enough crime scenes to know what one looks like. I'm sure the police are considering it a murder."

"And you believe it was?"

Ginger nodded. "You can't go through life making people miserable without somebody fighting back eventually. I suppose it could have just been a tussle and Lance slipped, but I don't think most people would choose a snow-covered roof to stage a fist-fight."

"Ginger, I hate to point out the obvious, but at least one person has already benefited from Lance King's death."

"You mean me. I know. Makes me look suspicious, doesn't it?" she said almost cheerfully. "But I never left your house. I stayed inside chatting with people. You have awfully nice neighbors, you know."

Jane shook her head. "You helped the other people with the crew take the equipment outside to set up."

Ginger didn't seem the least alarmed by this semi-accusation. "Oh, yeah. That's right. But I was with all the guys the whole time. Say, you don't really think—"

"No, I don't think you killed him. Although how you resisted the urge is beyond me. I'm just thinking out loud."

Ginger was sitting where she could see the drive-way. "Oh, a little red MG just drove in. Neat car."

"That's Detective VanDyne. And I'd be grateful if you'd let him in while I pull myself together."

Jane raced upstairs to dress and fling a comb through her hair. She could hear the shower running in the kids' bathroom and a quick peek in their rooms revealed that they were all still asleep so it must be Addie. It was another overcast day and her bedroom looked dreary. She opened the curtains to let what little sun there was come in and stared for a moment at the Johnsons' house next door. The ladder was still in place at the back and there were two men in the backyard. They drifted in and out of view and she couldn't tell what they were doing, but suspected they might be trying to fingerprint the ladder. She couldn't see the roof itself from her angle.

When she got downstairs again, Shelley was there and Mel appeared to be dismissing Ginger, who didn't want to be dismissed.

"Look, you're a witness and acquainted with the dead man," he explained. "As such, I need to know your movements and impressions. But you're also a reporter and you don't have any right to listen in on other people's reports. You should know the system. We'll tell you all we can without jeopardizing our investigation."

"Okay, okay," Ginger said grudgingly. "But it doesn't hurt to try, does it?"

She gathered up her coat, set her coffee cup in the sink, and left.

"What an irritating woman," Mel groused.

"Oh? I sort of like her," Jane said.

"Do you think she's truthful?"

"I don't know her well enough to guess. What were you asking her about?"

"Her movements and Lance King's work habits."

"Hard to think of what he did as work," Shelley put in. "What did she say?"

Mel got up and poured himself some coffee. "She

says he was very secretive about what he was investigating. She now remembers that he kept all his notes on computer disks, never put anything on the hard drive at his office or on his laptop. I wish she'd remembered that sooner. There were no documents on the laptop. Only his bookkeeping and some games."

"Games?" Jane asked. "He's the last person in the world I'd have expected to play any kind of games."

Mel ignored this observation. "I have a man checking his office computer, but it sounds like he's going to come up empty, too, if Ginger's right. She says he always kept his current disk on his person, but he didn't have it when he was found in the Johnsons' front yard."

"Somebody stole it?" Jane asked.

"Maybe," Mel said. "Or forced him to hand it over before pushing him off the roof."

"So whatever he was threatening to reveal about somebody is gone," Jane said. "I can't say I'm exactly sorry to hear that."

Shelley said, "But that means it's in someone else's hands. Someone who is capable of killing another person. Maybe somebody who's unethical enough to use the information King had on other people."

Eleven

"Jane, get a large sheet of paper, would you?" Mel asked. "I need you and Shelley to map out this block."

The only big sheet of paper Jane could find was the back of a piece of Christmas wrapping. "So you want a box for each house?" she asked, already sketching out squares.

"Number them, if you can," Mel said.

"Ooh," Shelley said. "We're doing police work on Santa wrapping."

Mel glared at her. "Not exactly," he said. "Just helping me get my bearings."

Jane had completed her boxes. "Mel, this one's vacant. The owners were transferred to Seattle before it sold." She put an X in the box and glanced at him.

He just nodded, still cranky about Shelley's remark.

Jane went on. "There are three older couples who couldn't come because they were going to be out of town visiting their children and grandchildren over the holidays."

"You're sure they were actually gone?" Mel asked.

"No, maybe not, but that's what they told me. I suppose it's possible they just made that up as an excuse, but it's not likely. The people in this house had tickets for the family to go to a musical last night," she said, entering another X. "And this one belongs to a couple of revoltingly fit yuppies who are spending the holidays in Bermuda. This one is Mrs. Eldridge, who was committed to have her bridge club at her house last night. I think those are most of the 'regrets' I got."

"Okay, now let's talk about who *did* come to the party and when."

"Well, the Johnsons, of course."

"The hillbillies next door?" Mel asked. "Were they here between eight-thirty and nine-thirty?"

"Why the times?"

"At eight-thirty I was watching Todd walk the little girl home," Mel said. "I looked at the Johnsons' decorations. No sign of a dead Santa and I'm sure I'd have noticed if there had been a struggle going on up on the roof."

"And at nine-thirty Julie discovered him," Jane added. "I see. I think the Johnsons were here the whole time. Billy Joe couldn't even walk through the house in his snowman costume without knocking things down. I can't imagine how he could have climbed a ladder in that outfit."

"Unless he removed it," Shelley said.

"Looked to me like it would have taken a helper to get him in and out of it," Jane said. "Didn't it button up the back? I think he and Tiffany were just too obvious to have sneaked out without being noticed."

"Why were they in costumes?" Mel asked.

Jane shrugged. "I have no idea. Maybe wherever they're from, a party always means a costume party. They obviously have a touch of exhibitionism about them, too, as you can tell from the house decorations."

"Okay, let's go house by house on the rest. Start at the corner."

"That's a couple with little kids who were, fortunately, at their grandparents' for the night or they might have brought them along. Terrors, those kids," Jane added. "One of them was actually kicked out of kindergarten for—"

"Jane!" Mel said sharply. "I don't care what the kid did in kindergarten. Were the couple here during the relevant time?"

"Yes, she was part of the crowd watching the movie. She has a real shrill laugh that I kept hearing. And he was in the basement with the guys."

Mel was taking notes. "Names?" he asked, and wrote down her reply. "Your basement doesn't have an outside entrance, does it?"

Jane shook her head. "You've seen my basement, Mel. No outside exit. Shelley, who were the other guys in the basement?"

Shelley reeled off a couple names, which Mel wrote down along with the rest of the movie-watching crowd. Jane marked off the book rep who'd been gossiping with Mel's mother, a single mother who brought along her new baby and wouldn't even let anyone else hold it, and a skier with a broken leg and crutches. They'd accounted for about three-quarters of the people on the block.

Mel ran his hand through his hair. "We'll have to confirm all of them, but at least I know who's at the bottom of the priority list. Now, what about the others? Whose house is this empty box?"

"Oh, that's our Julie Newton. The dim bulb who caused all this," Jane said.

"You know where Julie was during that hour?"

"Up in my bedroom calling security people," Jane said, embarrassed now by that loony idea.

"Your bedroom overlooks the Johnsons' house, doesn't it?" Mel said.

"Yes, I could see the top of the ladder poking up— Mel, you don't suspect Julie, do you?"

"Jane, my job is to suspect everyone. Do you know she was there? Could she have seen Lance King climbing the ladder?"

"I—I guess so. And she told me she couldn't get any security people to come out. I have no way of knowing if she actually called anyone or not. But Julie's such a flake!"

"Flakes have been known to kill people," Mel said. "I want to check out your bedroom window."

The three of them traipsed upstairs.

"Pretty good view in the daylight," Mel said, gazing toward the Johnson house. "And at night, with all the decorations lit up—there aren't any in the backyard, though. Is there a floodlight in back?"

Jane nodded. "My bedroom is lit up like a carnival at night from that window."

There was a light tap on the door and Addie walked in. "Oh," she said with mock surprise—which she didn't do very well. "I didn't know Mel was here," she said.

"And so am I, Mrs. VanDyne," Shelley said, coming out of Jane's bathroom where she'd been checking out the view from another window. Her grin was wicked.

Jane almost laughed. Addie must have heard them come upstairs and was checking out just what Mel was doing in Jane's bedroom in the middle of the morning.

Mel, of course, didn't get it. "Oh, hi, Mom. I thought you were sleeping in."

She laughed patronizingly. "You know I never sleep late. I'm so used to being up early to work."

Was that a dig at me? Jane wondered. *Or am I looking for digs?*

Shelley, Mel, and Addie went back downstairs and Jane stayed behind to bang on the kids' bedroom doors, alerting them that it was time to get up. If she let them start sleeping late this early in the vacation, they'd be staying up all night and keeping her awake.

When she rejoined the others in the kitchen, Mel and Shelley were sitting across from each other at the table, not speaking. It was a vaguely ominous silence.

"Mel's asking about Bruce Pargeter," Shelley said.

"Oh," Jane said, remembering the horrifying story of the sinkhole that he'd told them. She quickly weighed her options. Bruce hadn't sworn them to secrecy, nor would she have kept a secret that might have unraveled a murder. On the other hand, Bruce had implied that his family's story wasn't something he wanted spread around and she didn't want to spill it in front of Addie. It simply wasn't any of her business. Or anybody else's unless it was relevant to Mel's investigation.

She took a deep breath and said, "Mel, Bruce told us something about an experience he had with Lance King. I'm sure he'll tell you if you ask him. But I don't think Shelley and I have any right to blab about it unless he refuses to talk to you."

Addie, who was pouring herself a cup of coffee, spoke up. "Jane, my son is a detective investigating a serious crime—the murder of a man who had been in your house only a few minutes before his death. You haven't any right to withhold information from him."

Jane felt a violent flush crawling up her neck and heard Shelley's sharp intake of breath. But Mel saved them.

"Mom, Jane is being honorable. As she always is. Which is one of the many reasons I love her."

Jane started to get teary. Addie, however, gasped and turned pale at the word "love." She opened her mouth to speak, then snapped it shut, set her coffee cup down with exaggerated care, and marched out of the room and upstairs.

"She didn't know?" Shelley asked.

"I don't know how she couldn't," Mel said, confused by his mother's storm of emotion, repressed as it was.

Shelley mouthed, "Men!" and Jane smiled.

Mel wasn't fretting about his mother. He'd gone back to their map of the block. "Who's here? Oh, the little girl. What's her name?"

"Pet. Patricia Dwyer," Jane said.

"Why weren't her parents here? Or did they leave earlier?"

"Her father's a widower. Does something with computers and was working under a deadline, I guess. He didn't bother to respond to my invitation. Just didn't show up."

"She wasn't going home to an empty house, was she?" Mel asked, alarmed.

"No, she said he was working at home. I don't know if he has an office outside his house or not. He's terribly careful of her. That's why she has to be walked home after dark with an adult watching. And she can't accept rides. He even does those braids she wears. He's going to have a rough time when her hormones and independence kick in. He must be a good dad, but he's not much of a neighbor."

"I think maybe he's just awfully shy," Shelley said. "Sometimes shy people seem arrogant and aloof when they're really not."

"Didn't Suzie say she knew something about him?" Jane asked. "You might ask her about him."

Mel didn't seem too interested. He was studying his list. "I'm afraid of your friend Suzie," he said with a preoccupied half-smile. "Did you say she was in the basement with the men?"

"Naturally," Shelley said with a smile.

"And there's Ginger, of course, who isn't on the map," he mumbled as he fought to roll up the wrapping paper map. It had silly-looking Santas on the other side. Jane wondered why she'd ever bought it. *It's appropriate, in a way,* she thought, *but he's sure going to look ridiculous having it on his office desk.*

"What about the rest of his television crew?" Jane asked. "They had to spend a lot of time taking orders from him. He couldn't have been a pleasant person to work with."

"Three of them, and they alibi each other. Having coffee and doughnuts at the convenience store. The clerk said their van, which is pretty noticeable, was sitting in the lot the whole time. And none was foolish enough to pretend to have liked Lance. That *would* have made me suspicious."

Shelley was frowning. "I'm not so sure it has to be someone in the neighborhood. Nobody but Julie, Jane, and I knew she'd invited him. And he was promptly uninvited."

"Yes, but you know what a blabbermouth Julie is," Jane said. "She probably called all her friends on the block and carried on about her celebrity coup before she even dropped the bomb on me. And she's unlikely to have called them back to tell them I'd made her retract the invitation."

Mel stood up and gathered his paperwork. "I'm off to see your Mr. Pargeter."

"Good," Jane said cheerfully. "I have another party to hostess today."

"I guess I should tell Mom good-bye," Mel said.

"Is your furnace fixed yet?" Jane asked, rather pointedly, she feared.

"I don't know. Why do you ask? Mom's not being a nuisance, is she?"

"Oh, no. Not at all," Jane said with a false smile.

When he'd gone, Shelley said thoughtfully, "I think the Bible's wrong."

"The Bible?"

"Sure, the story is that God made Eve out of Adam's rib. I think God made Eve out of Adam's brains, which accounts for why men are men."

Jane laughed. "She's his mother, Shelley! Name me one man who can see through his mother."

"I can't. And you'd do well to keep that in mind."

Twelve

The kids finally stirred themselves, slouched downstairs, and messed up the kitchen fixing themselves breakfasts of varying degrees of sloppiness. Jane made Todd clean up the milk mess he'd made with his cereal, Katie the cookie crumbs, and Mike the granola bar wrapper. She'd done enough cleaning, washing up, and putting away last night after the caroling party that nothing remained to do before the cookie party except a little random tidying up. Jane vacuumed while Shelley put a fresh cloth on the dining room table. The kids had disappeared and Addie had not come back downstairs.

Jane and Shelley sat down in the living room. "If I had any sense, I'd be frantic at this point," Jane said.

"No need. Everything's under control."

"That's what's scary. It's the time everything seems to be under control that the plumbing backs up and the furnace goes out. It's a rule."

"Speaking of furnaces, and Mel's in particular," Shelley said, lowering her voice, "how long do you think you're going to have dear Addie here?"

"Not long, I hope. I want to like her, Shelley, and I just can't. She did a good job raising Mel, and I've got to admire her for that, but—"

"She doesn't want to let go of him?"

"That's my guess. Or maybe she just disapproves of me. And with good reason. I'm a couple years older than he is, I've got one grown-up son and two teenagers and no job, let alone a successful career or social position or any of the things women like in a daughter-in-law. You couldn't blame her for thinking I'm just looking for a husband to support me and help me with the kids and college tuition and all."

"Are you looking for a husband?" Shelley asked.

Jane stared at her. "Shelley, you astonish me. You're usually telling me what I think, not asking."

"So, I'm asking."

"I'm not looking for any old husband. These years since Steve died have been some of the best in my life. Well, that's got a lot to do with Steve's personality, I guess. But I'm pretty happy with things just the way they are and don't much miss washing a man's Jockey shorts and sorting his socks. I like having the closet and all the drawers in my bedroom

113

to myself and having a collection of books I'm reading all over the bed. It used to make Steve wild to crawl into bed and discover an Agatha Christie under his pillow."

Shelley's attention had wandered. "What are those strange noises upstairs?"

"Probably Mike moving stuff around. Or Katie rearranging her room for the eightieth time. Do you think we dare actually go out to lunch? The guests won't arrive until two. We could make it back in plenty of time to get the coffee started."

"I guess we'll have to invite Addie along," Shelley said glumly.

Jane sighed. "I guess so. With any luck, she'll turn us down."

Jane went upstairs and tapped lightly on the door to the sewing room. "Addie? Shelley and I are going to lunch and I wondered—"

She stopped speaking as Addie opened the door.

Jane came down a few minutes later, walking hard on her heels. "Let's go. Now," she said grimly.

Shelley knew the danger signs and quickly shoved her feet into her boots and grabbed her coat. A moment later, as they were getting into Shelley's car, which was parked in her driveway, Pet Dwyer tapped on Jane's window. Jane yelped with surprise and opened it.

"Mrs. Jeffry, you've having your cookie party today, aren't you?"

"I am," Jane said, "but I'm afraid kids aren't invited."

"But is my dad invited?"

Jane thought for a second. The neighborhood cookie parties had traditionally been girly-girly affairs, but times had changed. Pet's dad was just as much a single, stay-at-home parent as Jane herself was.

"Well, of course, Pet. I'm very sorry I didn't think to invite him sooner. We're just leaving, but I'll stop and ask him on the way."

"You don't need to. I'll tell him. He'll bring his fudge. He's making it now."

"If you'd rather, that would be fine," Jane said. She knew she should issue the belated invitation herself, but she was still too shaken by her recent encounter with Addie to take on another difficult person.

Pet waited safely and patiently while Shelley backed up in her usual hell-for-leather driving style. "I wonder if the idea of asking for an invitation was Pet's or her dad's?" Shelley said when they were on their way.

"Huh? Oh, good question," Jane said, preoccupied. "Sounds like it might have been his, since she said he was already making fudge. I really should have invited him without Pet prodding me to be polite."

They didn't speak again until they reached a little neighborhood Chinese restaurant that was one of their favorite spots to eat. It was barely eleven-fifteen and they were the first and only customers as yet. Luncheon was a buffet that was just being set out. Shelley ordered jasmine tea for both of them, then leaned forward and said, "Spill the beans, kiddo. What are you so pissed about?"

"She rearranged the sewing room. Actually moved the bed to the other wall and put the sewing table in front of the window."

"Addie moved a bed?"

"It's just a flimsy little bed and it's on rollers. But that's not the point. It's my house. My sewing room. I don't care that there's better light for sewing nearer the window. I had it like I liked it. I can't believe a woman of her sophistication would think that was acceptable guest behavior!"

"Oh, Jane! Get a grip! Of course she knows that. You're missing the point."

"Which is?"

"She's showing you what kind of mother-in-law she could be if you dare to marry her baby boy."

Jane stared at Shelley for a minute, then said, "You're right." Suddenly the whole incident struck her as funny. "She could have done worse. Dyed her hair and destroyed the bathroom. Or washed all my sweaters with bleach. I got off easy, I guess."

"You have to nip this in the bud, Jane, before she thinks of something else."

"Oh, I will," Jane said, grinning like a hyena.

Shelley cocked a shapely eyebrow, but didn't inquire further. She glanced at the buffet table. "Oh, look, they're bringing out that divine spicy beef and scallops thing!"

The two of them hardly talked during lunch, wolfing down their favorite Chinese food in a most unladylike manner. Finally, they sat back, sated and feeling stuffed and greasy.

Jane cracked open her fortune cookie. "'The wise man uses his time as if it were a treasure,'" she read. "Phooey! That's not a fortune, it's a homily. I want real fortunes in fortune cookies. Like, 'You will inherit vast sums of money in seventeen days,' or 'Your daughter will take good care of you when you get old and dotty and want to wear your panties on your head.' What's yours say?"

Shelley unfolded the little white strip of paper. "'Your son will get a full scholarship to Harvard.'"

"No! It does not," Jane said, snatching at the paper, which Shelley held just beyond her reach.

The waitress brought them a fresh pot of jasmine tea. Shelley checked her watch. "We don't need to leave quite yet. I wonder what they said on the noon news about Lance King's death?"

Jane shrugged. "Maybe that a celebration parade is being planned. How could anyone actually *want* to be disliked?"

"I think it goes back to fear. He knew he couldn't be liked, so he wanted to be feared instead. It gave him a sense of power. That was obvious. It's like hypochondriacs who think sympathy and love are the same thing," Shelley said.

"Got any ideas about whose button he pushed too hard?" Jane said.

"None," Shelley admitted. "But I want to know. If Mel's right, it's most likely someone in the neighborhood. Someone who needs to be scooped up and put in jail."

"I'm not so sure," Jane said. "There were a lot of people driving by and gawking at the Johnsons' house."

"But how many of them do you suppose said to themselves, 'Hey, there's Lance King, my life-long enemy, on a roof. Think I'll just give him a shove'? Besides, nobody driving by could have seen the ladder in back, much less guess that the guy on the roof *was* Lance King in a Santa suit."

Jane nodded. "You're probably right. Mel's probably right. I couldn't sleep well last night, trying to remember who was where and when," she said. "It was all just a blur though. I was so flurried that I hardly remember where I was, much less the rest of the guests."

Shelley sipped her tea. "I'm not sure it would have taken long enough for anyone to be missed. If somebody was trailing him, all they had to do was slip outside, wait until he had gone up the ladder, then follow him. One quick push was all it took, I assume."

Jane said, "But why would someone be following him just at that time? Surely he didn't mention that he was going to go climb on a dangerous, slippery roof. And he might just as well have gone to the television van with the other guys."

"Maybe somebody saw him climbing the ladder. Or

just saw him going between the houses. You can see that area from the side window in your dining room. No, I think alibis are going to be useless. It's the motive that's going to count and a lot of people had good reason to wish him dead."

"You're thinking about Bruce Pargeter?"

"Not seriously. But his name does come to mind."

"Only because he told us something about his background," Jane said. "Just think how many other people may have been hurt by the man and just don't talk about it."

Shelley glanced at her watch again. "I think maybe we better get going. You don't want to miss your own cookie party."

"Wanna bet?" Jane asked.

Thirteen

When they got home, Mel's MG was parked in the street and he was sitting in it, reading a report, which he hastily put away. "Was that the autopsy report?" Jane asked when he joined them at the kitchen door.

"Just a preliminary. Nothing unexpected. The metal support in the reindeer horn pierced his aorta. Death was nearly instantaneous. Other minor injuries that wouldn't have been life-threatening."

"How could anybody count on that happening?" Jane asked, taking off her coat and gathering up Shelley's and Mel's to put on the temporary rack.

"I don't suppose they could," Mel said. "This doesn't look like a well-thought-out plan—just someone taking advantage of a situation. Maybe it didn't matter if he died, just so he was injured enough to back off and leave someone alone."

"But what if he'd seen his attacker—and survived?" Jane asked. "Wouldn't it just make things that much worse?"

"I don't have the answer to that yet. I'm not sure we ever will unless we get an honest confession. It looks to me, from what little we know so far, like a sudden-impulse crime. Somebody who hated King, saw an opportunity to do him damage, and leaped at the chance without looking at the options."

"Sort of like that time you bought those stiletto heels, Jane," Shelley said with a grin. "No thought of the future or of the quality of the decision."

"Stiletto heels?" Mel asked.

"Never mind. I just meant we all do idiotic things on a whim occasionally."

"I'd hardly call murder a whim," Mel said.

It wasn't like Mel to be so stuffy, Jane thought. This case obviously wasn't going well for him. "No, what you're saying is that it was an act of passion, which is usually even more idiotic than a mere whim," Jane said.

"Speaking of whims," Mel said, "what have you done with my mother?"

"Dropped her off at the airport," Shelley said under her breath so he couldn't hear her, but Jane could.

"We invited her to lunch with us, but she said she didn't like Chinese," Jane replied. "I imagine she's still upstairs."

"It's the MSG that gets her," Mel said. "I guess I better take her someplace for lunch." He paused, waiting for them to let him off the hook.

Jane and Shelley smiled benevolently at him. Jane was tempted to say there were lots of leftovers they could eat, but kept quiet. She wanted Addie out of the house for a while. Just long enough to briskly move the sewing room furniture back to the way it had been before.

"Did you talk to Bruce Pargeter?" Shelley asked.

"Yes, at some length. He told me about the sinkhole, his father's decline and death after the scandal."

"And did he have an alibi for last night?" Jane asked.

"Sort of," Mel replied. "He says he told his mother about Lance King possibly being in the neighborhood and they decided to keep the lowest possible profile. His mother's bedroom and sitting room are at the back of the house. They turned off all the front lights, the mother went to her room, and Bruce spent the evening in the basement."

"In the basement? Hiding or what?" Shelley said.

"No, he's got a terrific woodworking shop down there. Said he was making a jewelry box for his mother's birthday next month. There were plans from a magazine and a half-done box. Incredibly fine work, by the way."

"So it wasn't something he whipped up this morning as an alibi?" Jane asked.

"Nope, but it doesn't prove anything. He could have done it a week ago and just *said* he worked on it last night. He's a nice guy, it seems, but I have nothing to convince me that he couldn't have been peering out a darkened upstairs window, saw Lance on the roof, and hared up the block to give him a push. His mother, without even being asked, admitted that she's a little hard of hearing and had the television in her sitting room turned up pretty loud."

"So he's a suspect?" Jane asked.

"Jane, at this point, everyone's a suspect. I've already been to do first interviews with all the people who were here, getting their impressions and asking them to make lists of times and people. By the way, 'Lance King' was a stage name."

"Was it? Who was he really?" Shelley asked.

"Harvey Wilhite."

"Wilhite?" Jane asked. "One of the neighbors is named Wilhite."

"Sharon Wilhite," Mel said. "Right. And she's his wife—ex-wife, rather."

"You're kidding!" Shelley exclaimed.

But before they could ask anything else, Addie Van-Dyne called down the stairs, "Mel? Is that you, dear?"

He went to meet her and a hurried, hissy conversation took place. Jane and Shelley strained their ears to overhear it, but couldn't get any sense out of the few words they could discern. "I'm going to run Mom out for lunch," he announced as he returned to the kitchen. He didn't look very pleased, Jane thought. Was it just that he resented taking precious time off the murder case or because of the content of their little whispered chat?

The minute Mel and his mother were out of sight, Jane and Shelley galloped upstairs. They put the bed back on the other wall and scooted the small work-table to the place it had formerly been. "Did she explain why she moved the furniture?" Shelley asked, neatly aligning the wastebasket under the table.

"No, neither of us mentioned it. I was too surprised to say anything that wasn't criminally rude."

They took a last look around and closed the door on the sewing/guest room.

"I feel just like a teenager who has just successfully TP'd a house!" Shelley said gleefully.

Suzie Williams was the first to arrive for the cookie party. She looked fabulous in an extremely well-fitted and well-underpinned green suit. The color made her greenish-blue eyes even more gorgeous than usual and her hair had been freshly platinumed. Suzie was a generous-sized woman with a sort of Mae-West-in-her-prime style. And the vulgar sense of humor to go with it. "I'm early. Sorry. But when you're in the girdle business, you've got to get while the getting is good."

"Suzie, what great cookies!" Shelley said with a little more enthusiasm than was strictly polite. Suzie's box contained several dozen little iced cookies that almost looked like miniature cakes. "Did you make these today?"

Suzie burst out laughing. "Not today, my dear. Not ever. They're straight from the bakery . . . you know, one of those places that makes your food for you. Nobody told me I had to *cook* the fucking cookies in order to come to this party."

"What bakery?" Shelley questioned, squinty-eyed. "I haven't found one that does such nice stuff."

While Suzie explained how to find the little, out-of-the-way bakery, Jane put her cookies on a serving plate. "Suzie, quick, before everybody else gets here, tell us about Whatsisname Dwyer," she said.

"Sam Dwyer," Suzie said. "I'd heard he was a widower and gainfully employed, which is enough for me to consider a man as a possible conquest. He was out in his yard one day last fall raking leaves, so I primped myself up and strolled down to chat with him. Tried to find out a bit about him, which wasn't easy because the man is a clam. But then, I'm good at opening clams. I finally got him to admit that his wife had died in a car accident when Pet was about three. Something about a road being flooded when a hurricane came through, so it was somewhere in the South. He didn't seem very sad about it and I got the impression that the marriage might have already been in trouble."

"Why is that?" Shelley asked.

"Oh, some comments he made later about how he really liked the quiet life he had here and how it was such a change. He's really pretty much of a confirmed hermit, I think, and she probably wanted a real high life—going out for dinner once a week to Denny's or something."

"What does he do for a living?" Jane inquired.

"Something with computer programs."

"Big help," Shelley said. "We knew that much."

"What can I say? Computers are a mystery to me," Suzie said. "Whatever it is, he does it at home. His main interest is Pet, though. He really adores that nerdy little girl. If a girl can be called a nerd. Went on about her terrific grades, how she never has to be told to clean her room, how smart she is about computers, and that she's already learning to cook."

"If her fudge is an example, she's got a way to go," Jane said. "Poor little Pet. What's going to happen when she 'blossoms' and wants to get free of him? It's great that he's such a devoted father, but there's trouble ahead."

"Well, it's not going to be my trouble," Suzie said.

"You've eliminated him from the marriage stakes?" Shelley asked.

"'Fraid so. In spite of the Mercedes in the garage."

"He drives a Mercedes?" Jane exclaimed.

"I don't think he actually drives it, just keeps it in his garage. I only saw it because he opened the garage door to put his rake away," Suzie said. "I've never seen him leave the house, have you?"

"Come to think of it, I haven't," Jane said. "Not that I pay much attention to who's coming and going.

125

Surely he has to go to the grocery store or the barber shop or something once in a while. He's coming to the cookie party, I think."

"No! Emerging from the clamshell to socialize?" Suzie said. "Amazing."

Jane's mother-in-law, Thelma, was the next to arrive. Thelma didn't live in the neighborhood and theoretically shouldn't have been included. But when Jane had inadvertently mentioned the plan, Thelma had assumed Jane was issuing an invitation and there was no way for Jane to retract it. Thelma might be the bane of Jane's existence, but she was also Jane's children's grandmother and hence, wasn't to be crossed any more often than necessary.

But today would be a landmark.

"Stay right here, you two," Jane ordered. "And agree with me—even if you don't."

Shelley and Suzie exchanged perplexed looks, but remained in the kitchen as Thelma entered. Both had met her a number of times and artificially cheerful greetings were exchanged. Then Thelma proceeded to do just what Jane had expected.

"Jane, dear, I have a little something for you," Thelma said, rummaging in her handbag and fishing out a check. This was a temporary triumph for Thelma. She always liked delivering the monthly check in front of an audience if she could manage it.

Although Thelma liked to be Lady Bountiful in this scenario, bestowing what she pretended was a generous gift, it wasn't a gift at all. Jane's husband, his brother, Ted, and his mother, Thelma, had jointly owned a small chain of pharmacies. Early in Jane and Steve's marriage, there had been a severe financial crunch and Jane had contributed a small inheritance to the pharmacies to help keep the business afloat. Steve had insisted that under the circumstances, a contract would be drawn up to make his third of future profits Jane's as well. So, though Steve had been dead for years now, Jane was still entitled to her one-third share. Steve hadn't intended to die, of course. The contract was pure sentiment—a means of thanking his then-new wife.

But since his death, Thelma had performed the monthly ritual of giving Jane her check as though it were a present—out of the goodness of her heart. And as the years went on, Jane had become more resentful and humiliated with each presentation. But from now on, things would be different. It was Jane's own gift to herself.

She took the check from Thelma, folded it neatly, and put it in her pocket. With a smile, she said, "Thelma, that's the last time you will need to put yourself out this way."

"What do you mean?" Thelma said brightly, apparently thinking Jane meant to forgo her share of the profits.

"I talked to the bank this week and arranged to have the funds transferred automatically to my account." This wasn't strictly true. The pharmacy's accountant would have to approve it, but Jane would talk to him later. "You won't even have to bother with the check anymore."

Thelma was taken completely off-guard. "But Jane, I *like* giving you the check," she said.

Jane kept her smile frozen in place. "I know you do, but I don't like it, Thelma. This will work out much better."

Shelley threw herself into the momentary silence while Thelma was gathering her wits for a riposte. "Jane, what an excellent idea that is! How very considerate of you to save Mrs. Jeffry the trouble of hand-delivering it. And how much easier it will make the bookkeeping."

Suzie, who had no idea of what the underlying current was, but recognizing that it was in full flood, contributed, "I have my paycheck done that way. Straight into the bank electronically. Saves all the concern about a check ever getting lost. And it's a lot easier for me and the company at tax time. All the transactions are recorded automatically and a machine just spits them out in January."

"But—" Thelma stuttered.

"It will be better for everyone this way," Jane said firmly. Very firmly.

The doorbell rang and Jane said, "Oh, more of our guests," as she left the kitchen. She paused in the front hall and did a quiet little victory dance before opening the door wearing a manic smile.

Fourteen

Two of the older ladies on the block were at the door, looking rather alarmed by Jane's excessively enthusiastic welcome. Jane saw Mel pulling into the driveway to deliver his mother. Jane ushered in the two neighbors and took their coats and cookie boxes and heard Shelley, in the kitchen, introducing Addie Van-Dyne to Thelma Jeffry. *Wonder what they'll make of each other,* Jane thought. *Mincemeat, most likely.*

Mel left without even coming in the house. Jane hurriedly set more cookies out on trays and waited at the front door for the next guests. A clump of ladies all converged at the same time. One of them was Sharon Wilhite. Jane was eager to get her aside and question her about Lance King, but not in front of the mob of cookie-bearing neighbors.

The party showed every sign of being a grand success. The dining room table was laden with trays of cookies—everybody's most elaborate recipes. Spritz cookies with fancy shapes and Christmas colors, date-roll cookies, tiny iced nutmeg logs, gingersnaps, rum balls—a cornucopia of sugary delights. The house smelled of pine boughs and hot cinnamon cider and the rich scent of the Godiva coffee Jane practically had to take a loan out to purchase.

It put last night's disastrous party out of Jane's mind. This was a good neighborhood party, a celebration of the holidays without a threat in their midst. Unless, of course, one of these women had hoisted herself up the ladder—no, she wouldn't let herself think about that right now.

Tiffany Johnson arrived by herself, clad in an ill-fitting red organdy-over-taffeta frock that was obviously expensive and totally inappropriate. Jane went out of her way to make Tiffany welcome, although the woman obviously hadn't clued in that she was seriously overdressed for the occasion. She'd brought along exquisite puff pastries with a dusting of powdered sugar, which surprised Jane. She'd expected Tiffany to turn up with something heavy, filling, and distinctly "down home" instead of something so fine and delicate.

Shelley strolled into the dining room, looking over her shoulder at Tiffany. "I don't get it, Jane."

"Don't get what?"

"The Johnsons. That's a very pricey dress Tiffany's wearing. Awfully mother-of-the-bride-ish, but good quality. Where do they get the money? How do they afford the rent on their house? Do they *do* something for a living?"

"I have no idea," Jane said. "The only thing I can figure is that they inherited a wad from some distant relative."

"Or maybe Billy Joe sold out a highly successful hog-butchering factory," Shelley said.

"They aren't as ignorant as you'd think," Jane said. "I meant to tell you about this. I went over to invite

Tiffany to the parties and Billy Joe was working away at a computer."

"Probably just playing a game."

"No, I don't think so. I caught a glimpse of the room before Tiffany hastily closed the door. There were shelves of books and computer manuals."

"Jane, when you're past this entertaining binge, we have to try to find out more about them. You can't entirely overlook the fact that Lance was killed at their house. Could just be a random roof he chose, or it could be more."

"You mean Lance knew about them?"

"Possibly. He was even nosier than we are."

"But Shelley, that doesn't make sense. If he were setting up a 'spy station' to spy on them, he'd have been on someone else's roof, wouldn't he?"

"Let me think that over," Shelley said as the doorbell rang.

Another group arrived together and the noise level went up significantly. Of course, they were having to compete with Billy Joe Johnson's Christmas music which was once again blasting the neighborhood. Jane was strolling through the living room, greeting friends and feeling smug when a relative silence fell over the room. Everybody was gazing at the doorway to the kitchen, where Sam Dwyer stood, looking very awkward.

"You must be Sam Dwyer. How nice that you could join us," Jane said. "Ladies, this is Sam Dwyer. Pet's dad. You'll all have to introduce yourselves."

The noise level gradually climbed again as Jane took the box Sam had brought along. "Oh, what lovely fudge," she said. It was a huge improvement on the fudge Pet had brought the day before.

"Thank you," Sam said quietly. "Where should I put it?"

"Come along to the dining room," Jane said, leading the way and handing him one of the brightly colored plastic serving trays. While he moved the squares of fudge onto the tray, she studied him. She'd never gotten a close look at him before, just a general impression from down the block. He was better-looking than she would have guessed from a distance. His hair was too short to be stylish and his glasses were a bit on the Buddy Holly side, but his features were strong and handsome. He wore a charcoal gray tweed jacket with suede elbow patches, a light gray shirt and tie, and black dress slacks. Very well turned out for a computer nerd.

"I appreciate all you've done for Pet," he said, setting the last piece of fudge in place.

"I haven't done anything for her. Except enjoy her. She's a nice little girl. A credit to you."

"You're more important to her than you know. She's shy around most people, but feels comfortable coming to your house and being friends with your son. She told me you even let them use your computer."

Jane was surprised at the compliments. "They both know more about computers than I do. I don't worry that they'll wreck it as much as I worry that I will."

"Well, I still want to thank you for making her feel that your house is sort of a second home. We don't have family here and it's pretty lonely for her at home sometimes. I'm her only companion there and my work takes a lot of my time and concentration. She really enjoys your family. She's always telling me about how busy and interesting everybody in the Jeffry family is."

"Listen, Sam, any man who is able and willing to do tidy French braids is a fine dad."

He laughed. "I keep hoping she'll get interested in doing them herself!"

Thelma came into the dining room just then. She gave them an appraising look and said, "Jane, is there anything I can do to help?"

Jane introduced Thelma to Sam and said, "No, I think everything's under control. There are two more people I believe are coming. We'll give them another five minutes before turning everybody loose on the cookie distribution."

Thelma gave Sam another close look. She appeared to be faintly disapproving of his presence as an invited guest, but since she was faintly disapproving of most things Jane did, this wasn't surprising.

"You live here on the block, Mr. Dwyer?" Thelma asked.

"Yes, in the blue house down the street and across. My daughter Pet is a friend of Todd's."

He was smiling slightly and Jane suspected that he knew Thelma was dying to grill him about his presence among the women on the block. "I think maybe I should meet some more of my neighbors," he said.

When he'd left the room, Thelma said, "What is he doing here? I didn't think men were invited."

"He's a single, stay-at-home parent, Thelma. A widower. He hasn't been very sociable until now. I think it's nice that he came."

"I suppose it is, but it's certainly odd. What's this I hear about Lance King?" she asked with an abrupt shift. "I heard some of your other guests talking about his death. I didn't have time to read the paper this morning and didn't know."

"He fell off the roof next door and died," Jane said bluntly.

"But someone said he'd just been here. In *your* house."

"Unlike Sam Dwyer, Lance King was not here at my invitation, Thelma."

"What was he doing on the neighbors' roof?"

"Snooping, apparently. Scouting for a place for setting up a camera or listening device possibly."

"Dreadful man!" Thelma said. "Not that one wishes dreadful people to die, of course. Still, he was a terrible person. Always going after people who couldn't defend themselves against him. I lived in fear—" She stopped.

"That he'd go after the family pharmacies?"

"No, of course not." She paused. "Well, yes. Not that we had anything to really fear, but he seemed to just make things up, just to stir the pot."

"He did, indeed."

"So he just fell off the roof?"

Jane debated with herself for a moment. Surely the newspaper or television reporters had already gotten wind of the fact that Lance King was probably murdered. After all, the bright yellow crime scene tapes around the Johnsons' house were pretty much of a tip-off. No point in keeping Thelma in the dark. "I don't think he managed it by himself," Jane said.

"What do you mean?"

"That it's likely that he was pushed off the roof."

Thelma gasped. "Murdered? Right next door to you?"

"Better there than here," Jane said.

"Oh, Jane. Don't even say such a thing. I had no idea! Who did it? Who killed him?"

"I don't know. The police are investigating."

Thelma shifted gears again. "Jane, I want to talk to you about this business about your monthly check—"

Fortunately, Shelley interrupted at exactly the right moment. "I think everybody's here, Jane. They're all stoked up on cider and coffee. Want me to invite them to eat?"

"Yes! But I'll do it," she said, frantic to escape Thelma. She'd spent most of a week gearing herself up for the earlier confrontation, but wasn't ready for another round.

Everyone was full of praise for Jane's table and the variety of goodies. Jane had tiny plates set out for sampling the sugary feast. Later everyone would be given pretty little boxes to take home a mixture of cookies. Jane was sorry the tradition had been allowed to lapse for several years and glad that she'd been the one to revive it. While the guests were gushing and choosing, she went into the living room. As she passed by the stairs, Addie was just coming down. She started to say something, thought better of it, and merely nodded to Jane with a faint, artificial smile. Jane smiled back.

Shelley was sitting by herself on the sofa. Jane joined her and whispered, "Addie's just been upstairs."

Shelley grinned. "Did she say anything?"

"Not a word."

They giggled like schoolgirls.

"It's such a joy to see you enjoying your own party," Catherine Pargeter said, sitting down awkwardly in the squishy armchair. "Oh, dear, it's probably going to take a crane to get me back out of here."

Catherine was in her late fifties, a bit on the heavy side, and was vaguely grandmotherly, although she had no grandchildren. She had the same fair hair and ruddy complexion as her son Bruce. Jane didn't know her terribly well, but liked her. Catherine was deeply, seriously into genealogy and when Jane and Shelley developed an interest in the subject, Catherine had been more than willing to answer their very stupid, beginner questions. And she did so with good cheer and grace.

"I was sorry you couldn't come to the party last night," Jane said. "Although it didn't turn out to be very festive."

"I just couldn't, dear. Not with the threat of that awful man being here. I can't say I'm glad he's dead, but I can't say I'm sorry, either. Bruce told me he explained it all to you and Shelley."

"He did and it broke my heart," Jane said sincerely.

"It's a long time ago. One can't dwell on heartache," Catherine said. Then she brightened in a deliberate manner. "How are you getting along with your genealogy, Shelley?"

While Shelley and Catherine chatted, Jane watched as the others drifted back to the living room. Addie and Thelma were in conversation again, both of them still looking a bit cranky. Since the only thing they had in common was Jane herself, she was glad to be spared hearing them. Sam Dwyer had been cornered by Julie Newton. Julie's bouncy perkiness seemed to disconcert him. He almost flinched every time she made one of her grand gestures—and she was making a lot of them. Sharon Wilhite and Tiffany Johnson were trying to find some everyday subject for conversation and apparently finding it heavy going. One would speak and the other would look interested but perplexed. Then they'd reverse the process. Then, as Jane observed them, they both laughed. Apparently the death of the ex-husband of one woman, the site of that death being the home of the other, hadn't really harmed either of them.

If Lance King were looking down (or up, more likely) on this scene from wherever his mean spirit had gone, he must have been severely disappointed at how little his passing had meant.

Fifteen

The guests started drifting off around three-thirty and Jane was reminded of one of the things she'd always loved about the cookie parties. Everyone always brought a lot more cookies than they were supposed to and took away only a few more than specified, with the result that the hostess ended up with a hearty supply of everyone else's baking efforts. She'd probably gain ten pounds by New Year's, but what was January good for except dieting?

Jane stood at the door, hugging an afghan around her shoulders to keep warm, bidding everyone good-bye, making sure they had the right hats, gloves, boots, and their box of cookies. Mel arrived again as the last stragglers departed. "Hi, Janey," he said brightly. "Guess what?"

She grinned at him. He'd cheered up considerably since the last time she'd talked to him. "Okay . . . you got a raise? A Christmas bonus? An Oscar for being *my* leading man?"

"You aim too high, Janey," he said, giving her a light peck of a kiss. "I got my furnace fixed. On a Saturday!"

It was all Jane could do to keep from shouting, *"WHOOPEE!"* "On a Saturday," she said calmly. "Imagine that."

"So I can take Mom off your hands."

Jane could afford to be gracious now. "Oh, she hasn't been a bit of trouble, Mel."

"Oh—well. Maybe she'd rather stay here, then."

"No, no, no! I mean, I'm sure she wouldn't. She came to see you, Mel. Not camp out here with all the kids and noise."

Men could be such dim-bulbs about their mothers.

Addie, still deep in conversation with Thelma, was informed that she was moving and went upstairs to pack. *And probably to have another shot at moving the furniture,* Jane thought. Shelley saw to it that Thelma was levered out the door without getting another chance to take Jane to task about the Great Check Delivery Debate and was in the kitchen putting soiled plastic plates and cups into a trash bag when Mel and Jane joined her.

"Excellent party, Jane," Shelley said, giving the trash bag an expert twirl and closing it up with a plastic gizmo. "Almost no mention of the late and not very lamented Lance King."

"It *was* a nice party, wasn't it?" Jane said. "Mel, I've got a ton of leftover cookies. Want some?"

"Just to help you out."

"Speaking of Lance King, how's it going?" Shelley asked.

"Not well. Not well at all. Ginger must be right

about him keeping everything on disk. There was nothing on the laptop of any use. I guess I told you that. And there wasn't anything on his office machine except a word processing program with files identified by date, but without any content."

"Without content?" Jane asked.

"Empty as a baton twirler's head," Mel said.

"Watch it or some feminist group will come after you," Shelley warned him. "I'll have you know that I, Shelley Nowack, once took baton twirling lessons. Well, one lesson."

"Not much good at it?" Jane asked.

"I gave myself a bloody nose with the knob on the end and my mother threw the baton away," Shelley admitted. "Seriously, Mel, aren't you making any progress?"

"I didn't say that. We're still gathering evidence, doing interviews. Time-consuming, but necessary."

"I don't guess you're going to tell us who you suspect?" Shelley said.

"Nope. Because I suspect everybody at the moment."

"Suspect everybody of what?" Addie said from the doorway.

"Suspect everybody of everything," Mel said cheerfully. "Are you ready to go? I'll get your bag."

Addie had a lot of lovely things to say about Jane, her children, and her house and emphasized how extraordinarily kind it had been of Jane to take her in.

Jane gushed about what a very welcome guest she had been and how pleasant it had been to get to know her, even though things had really been too hectic for a good heart-to-heart.

Behind Addie and Mel, Shelley was making gagging motions.

Addie and Jane parted with warm enthusiasm and anticipation of their next meeting which would once again be at Jane's house for Christmas a few short days away. How time does fly. Air kisses were exchanged. Artificial laughter filled the air. Fake smiles beamed.

As soon as Mel and his mother had backed out of the driveway, Jane shuddered elaborately and said, "I hate myself."

Shelley had her head down on the kitchen table, howling with laughter. "You should. That was the most disgustingly gooey scene I've seen since *Love Story*."

"Don't worry. Mel's the only one who didn't understand it," Jane said. She sat down and propped her feet on another chair. "Thank God, my entertaining is over for a few days. The Christmas Day dinner looms ominously, but I'm not thinking about it until tomorrow at the earliest."

"You're not quite done. Sharon Wilhite brought her cookies on her own tray and left it behind. We need to take it back to her."

"And ask a few questions?" Jane said.

"Oh . . . maybe just a few."

Jane had never been in Sharon's house and was surprised at how tastefully bland it was. Sharon apparently subscribed to the "Beige Is Good" school of decorating. There were bits of color here and there. A muddy blue vase. A rug with charcoal and cream colors. An abstract painting over the sofa that had hints of apricot with the beige. It was a house that wasn't really lived in very much. There was no clutter, no newspaper or *TV Guide.* In fact, no television that Jane could see.

Though Shelley claimed they'd only stopped by to deliver Sharon's platter (as if it took two of them to carry it), Sharon wasn't fooled. "I guess I owe you an explanation," she said.

"You don't owe it, but I'd sure like to hear it anyway," Jane said.

"Do you smoke?" Sharon said unexpectedly.

"Sometimes. As little as possible," Jane replied.

"Feel free then."

"I didn't bring any along. It's okay," Jane said.

"I'll get you a cigarette. I used to smoke and keep one pack in the house just so I don't panic." She opened a little drawer under the coffee table and got a pack out. She was obviously hedging, thinking what to say.

"No thanks, I'm fine," Jane said, recognizing a brand that had changed its packaging a good five years earlier. She didn't mind stale, but objected to petrified. And she wanted Sharon to get on with what she had to say.

Jane and Shelley settled themselves on the sofa,

while Sharon chose a straight-backed chair with a beige and brown seat cover. "I married Harvey—Lance, that is—in college. It was partly an escape from my parents, partly a general rebellion, partly sex. He was interesting. Most of the guys who were attracted to me were jocks. Harvey was an intellectual. Not really, but he gave that impression to a girl as foolish and lonesome as I was. It only lasted a year."

"Who got dumped?" Shelley asked bluntly.

"Oh, I dumped him. I wasn't entirely stupid. I found out that he was—well, 'wicked' sounds melodramatic, but he was wicked. Or sociopathic. He was always bragging about the things he'd put over on people. That made me uncomfortable, but I told myself it was just made up. Jokes, you know, to see how I'd react. I always just laughed it off. Then one day he said something about how silly it was for me to be paying college fees. Told me he could hack into the university computer and show my tuition as paid. This was in the early days of computers. He didn't have his own, but had access to one in a science lab. He proceeded to explain that he'd only paid his first-semester tuition and had gotten his education for free since then."

Sharon fiddled with the ancient cigarette pack for a minute before continuing. "And he'd fooled around with his grades, too. Given himself straight A's and credit for courses he hadn't even taken. I was young and stupid and thought I could get through to him about why this was wrong, wrong, wrong. But he kept talking. Told me about some of the other students he'd 'fixed.' That was the word he used. He'd created his own 'enemies' list—people he imagined had crossed him in some way. He'd done the opposite with them. Lowered their grades, deleted courses. That's when I knew I had to get away from him."

"Were any of the neighbors on the 'enemy' list?" Shelley asked.

"I don't know. It was so long ago and he only mentioned first names. When their grades came out, I'm sure it was just blamed on some kind of mysterious computer error anyway," Sharon said.

"Not if he bragged to other people as well as you," Jane said.

"Still, I can't imagine anyone holding a grudge over a grade for fifteen years or more and then killing someone over it, can you?"

"No, I guess not. So you divorced him?"

Sharon nodded. "But I got several notarized printouts of my college transcript first," she said with a smile. "I was getting smarter by the minute. I used those to apply to other schools so that it wouldn't show on my record where I'd asked for copies to go, then I filed the divorce papers and left him."

"Is that when you came here?" Jane asked.

"No, I finished my undergraduate courses in Vermont and got my law degree in Massachusetts. Then I got a job here. I wasn't deliberately moving around, it just worked out that way. But what I didn't realize is that he was sort of stalking me. I don't think the word was in common use then, but that's what he was doing. One day about three years ago, he turned up on my doorstep. I'd worked with a firm that had a branch in Kentucky and somehow he spotted my name in the property records."

"Did he threaten you?" Shelley asked.

"Oh, no. Not directly. Just said he'd changed, turned his 'curiosity,' as he called it, to good ends—exposing graft and corruption and dishonesty. And that he thought I'd like him better now and we might as well get back together. He'd followed me to Chicago and gotten a job with a local television station so we could be together."

She shuddered at the memory.

"What did you do?" Jane asked.

"Nothing for a while. I'd put on a bit of weight, gotten rather stuffy and dull and I thought he'd give up and go away. But he didn't. He called every day. I got frightened."

"Of course you did. Did you call the police?"

"Yes, but it didn't do much good." The cellophane wrapper on the cigarette pack was in shreds now. "He'd made no overt threats, didn't break into my house or anything like that. He wasn't a clear danger to me from their viewpoint, only a nuisance. And I suppose, in a way, they were right. I don't honestly think he'd have committed any physical violence. Just psychological and financial. Every time I booted up my computer at work, I could imagine him hunched over his, tapping into my life and the life of my clients. At least some good came of it," she said with a smile. "I insisted that the law firm get the most 'hacker-proof' computer system we could find."

"Why did you come to the caroling party then?" Shelley asked. "Surely you'd heard that there was a possibility that he'd turn up there."

"Because Julie told me that he wasn't coming after all. And besides, I thought I'd gotten rid of him," Sharon said. "After about six months of trying to fend him off, I told him I'd recorded his remarks about cheating the university and changing his grades and other people's and if he didn't leave me alone, I'd turn over a copy to the television station and insurance carrier."

"He believed it?" Shelley asked.

"Not quite, but I was a lot smarter by then and a much better liar. I did have a tape recorder at the time that I used a lot. I told him I'd been planning to divorce him for a long time and had recorded many of our conversations just in case he decided to contest the divorce action. Went on to explain that I'd made copies of the tapes, put them in my safe deposit box along with a notarized, dated transcript done by another attorney. I really spread myself thin on the story. I blabbed about how I had a client who said a competing television station was considering getting their own 'action reporter' and mentioned what a coup those tapes would be for them as their first story."

"You're good!" Jane exclaimed.

"It seemed to work," Sharon said modestly. "I don't

think he entirely believed me, but he couldn't take the chance of losing his nasty little career. I didn't hear from him again. But there was something else that I couldn't undo . . ."

"Which was?" Shelley asked.

"During the time he was bugging me, he decided he could exert pressure on me by investigating my friends and neighbors. Nothing he could be prosecuted for, just hints. 'So-and-so's been divorced three times; wonder if his wife knows that?' he'd say. Or 'Such-and-such has a couple shoplifting arrests in her past. Isn't that interesting?'"

Jane had been leaning forward, listening intently. Now she flopped back on the sofa and exchanged a look with Shelley. "That answers one question, doesn't it? Shelley and I were wondering how he could get invited to the party one day and pretend to have an exposé on the neighborhood ready by the next day. He already had material!"

"Have you told the police all this?" Shelley asked sharply.

"Of course I have," Sharon said. "I have nothing to conceal and no sympathy for Harvey or the person who killed him—whoever that was."

"I presume you're not going to tell us who he said these things about," Jane said. "And frankly, I don't think you should. But you did tell the police, right?"

Sharon nodded. "I told them what little I could remember. But I was so disgusted with most of the junk he told me that I made a real effort to put it out of my mind and a few of the things I do recall were about people who have moved away."

"So you have no idea who might have killed him?" Jane asked.

"None. And I don't care."

The pack of cigarettes was open now and she was rolling one of them between her fingers.

Sixteen

"Do we believe her?" Shelley asked as they walked back to her house.

"I'd like to," Jane replied, "but she admitted she was a good liar. Maybe she's lying to us and the police about her marriage and background."

"It makes sense," Shelley said. "If it's a lie, it's an elaborate, well-thought-out one. It might be that most of it is true, but parts aren't."

"Which parts?"

Shelley said, "I have no idea. But did you notice how calm her voice was—and all the while she was ripping into that pack of historical cigarettes? Let's assume she's telling mostly the truth. The weak points are, first, that she did get rid of him like she said, but then he started harassing her again and she killed him."

"I don't think she was dressed for it," Jane said.

"Dressed for murder? You mean she wasn't wearing a Ninja outfit?"

"No, she had on heels and a fairly tight skirt the night he was killed. It would be damned hard to hoist yourself up an icy ladder in that getup."

"But not impossible," Shelley said. "Her boots were probably in the front hall of your house. Put them on, dash outside, hitch up the tight skirt. Yeah, yeah. Unlikely."

"What's the next weak point she could be lying about?"

"Not knowing who her ex-husband had the dirt on. Or not remembering. That doesn't ring true. If you told me Mrs. Whatsis down the street was the head witch of a coven, I'd sure remember it for a long time."

"But Shelley, we're snoops—"

"No, we're curious women who are concerned with the welfare of our friends," Shelley said.

Jane didn't quibble. "Okay, we're curious, but what's more important, we actually know most of the neighbors. She doesn't seem to be really chummy with much of anyone because she's gone so much of the time. It wouldn't be too surprising if she didn't recall the dirty details years later about someone she never even met or heard of before."

They'd reached Jane's house. "Paul is taking the kids to a fast-food dinner and a movie tonight," Shelley said. "I don't have to fix dinner. Can you fling some edibles at your kids and we could go eat together?"

"My kids are stuffed to the gills with leftover

cookies. They probably won't even consider food for hours. It's not quite five yet. Let's go now. I'll make sure of where they are and what they're doing and be over in a minute."

Jane went in the kitchen door and was heading upstairs to refresh her makeup when Katie called down the steps, "Hey, Mom, did you see the boxes?"

"What boxes?" Jane turned and looked toward the front door. Three or four battered cardboard cartons were piled up. "Oh, that must be the stuff from your grandparents. They've been fretting about them not arriving in time."

"Can we open them?"

Jane continued up the steps. "Sure. They always wrap the individual gifts inside the big boxes. Put the gifts under the tree. And no peeking or shaking."

"You're not going to lecture me again about that little china tea set I broke when I was a little kid, are you?"

"Any second now. You guys aren't hungry yet, are you?"

Katie blew up her cheeks and shook her head. "Food—yuck!"

"Then I'm going to go out with Mrs. Nowack. How about I bring back barbequed ribs?"

Jane took their dinner orders and hurried to Shelley's house. The kids had stuffed themselves with cookies, but she hadn't had any and lunch was a long time ago. She was starving. Shelley already had her car warming up in the driveway.

"Since we still look fairly decent, let's go someplace kind of nice," Shelley suggested.

There was a new French restaurant a couple miles away they'd been wanting to try, but hadn't pulled themselves together and put on panty hose and heels to give it a shot yet. Once again, they were almost the only customers because they were so early. A very handsome young waiter in a tuxedo seated them, actually holding their chairs and flipping open generously sized blue napkins that he laid reverently on the women's laps.

"Wow!" Jane whispered when he left to get their menus. "I could get used to this. Especially if all the waiters look like him."

He was back in a moment with the menus, which were leather-bound and enormous. He had another server with him, this one in a short white jacket. He carried a silver tray with two exquisite goblets of water. The waiter explained the specials of the day with loving purple prose and a lot of French terms Jane should have understood and didn't.

"What are those in English?" she asked.

"Translated loosely," he said, lowering his voice, "meat loaf and stew. But the best meat loaf or stew that you'll ever taste."

"Shelley, let's have one of each. And we could trade."

"Jane, we do not pass food back and forth here," Shelley hissed. "Your parents would have strokes if they heard you suggesting something so gauche."

"I could give you each a half order of both," the waiter suggested.

"You're a good man," Jane said. "And why don't you just give us a wine you recommend so I won't feel silly about ordering it?"

That got him to crack a smile.

When he was out of earshot, Jane leaned forward and said quietly, "These fancy plates on the table— chargers, I think they're called?"

"What about them?"

"Well, nobody ever eats on them. They take them away when they serve dinner, so do they have to be washed?"

Shelley stared at her for a long moment and said, "Have you considered psychiatric care?"

"I just wondered. They've got this nice gold rim, so they couldn't be put in a dishwasher and it seems a waste of time and effort to make people wash them by hand when nobody's ever eaten off them."

Shelley rolled her eyes and said, "Wonder about Sharon Wilhite instead. She said she'd told the police everything she told us. I imagine that's true. She must know you're involved with Mel. He was at the party."

"Do you think she even noticed? Come to think of it, it must be a blot on his copybook to have someone murdered practically under his nose. I'll call and ask him this evening if Sharon told him the same thing."

"Wonder why he didn't tell us?" Shelley said as the

white-jacketed server whisked away the ashtray that Jane had put only a speck of ash in and replaced it with a fresh one.

"For one thing, he's not really supposed to tell us anything about an investigation, although he sometimes does. For another, there really hasn't been any chance to talk with him without Addie barging in."

"Say, that's interesting," Shelley mused. "He does tell us some things he probably shouldn't. But he doesn't want to talk about them to Addie. Indicates a relative scale of trust, huh?"

Jane smiled. "Maybe. Or he just knows she's not interested. If Sharon told him what she told us, I imagine he has ways of checking the main facts—like where they went to college, when each of them moved here. Stuff like that."

"Jane, we didn't order appetizers."

"Talk about priorities!" Jane said with a laugh.

Shelley had barely time to turn and look for the handsome waiter before he appeared as if by magic. He suggested an order of buttered, toasted French bread rounds with pâté, and another of broiled eggplant with a lemon and garlic sauce.

After that, Shelley and Jane turned their attention from murder to food.

"Why didn't you even let me see the bill?" Jane asked as they departed an hour later. "I would have at least done the tip."

"You don't want to know what it cost. Take my word

for it. But after two parties back-to-back, you deserve to be treated."

Knowing how very much money the Nowacks had and how stingy Shelley usually was with it, Jane accepted the fact that Shelley was right.

Jane came in the house via the kitchen a few minutes later, put the carry-out food on the kitchen table with some paper plates left from the caroling party, and went to yell up the steps. She tripped over a pile of rubble. Boxes and pink Styrofoam peanuts were all over the hallway.

"Hey, guys! Your food is here," she bellowed. "And you can have it when this mess is cleaned up."

"Sorry, Mom," Katie said, bounding down the stairs. "We forgot. Oh, and we made a mistake. We assumed all the boxes were gifts and ripped into one that's not even meant for us. I don't know why the mailman left it here."

"Where was it supposed to go?"

"To those people next door. The Johnsons."

"Okay, Mike can take the box over and explain when you've got the rest of this tidied up."

Jane changed into comfortable clothes, fended off a telephone call from a roofing and siding company ("You're calling me on Saturday night?"), and went downstairs with the full intention to spend a mindless evening in front of the television, or maybe playing gin on her laptop.

The debris in the front hall was gone. All but the gaping box of books that belonged to the Johnsons.

Jane bent over to see what kind of books they were and discovered that they were all the same book. Why would the Johnsons be getting what appeared to be a couple dozen of the same title? Good Lord, did they intend to go door-to-door selling them or something?

She picked one up, read the cover copy, flipped through a few pages, then turned it over. The couple who wrote the book were pictured on the back. She glanced at the picture and set the book back in the box. She headed for the living room, but came to a dead halt in the doorway. She returned to the box, took one of the books back out, and carried it into the kitchen where the light was better. She studied the photo on the back again.

"Kids, I'll be back in a minute. Just running over to the Nowacks'. Don't anybody touch that box of books until I get home."

Shelley was already in her nightgown and robe. "You again?" she said with a smile.

"I want to show you something," Jane said, coming into Shelley's disgustingly clean kitchen. She handed Shelley the book.

"Oh, yes. I didn't know this was out yet. I've seen a couple of excellent reviews of it. You've read these people before, haven't you?"

"I don't think so," Jane said.

"Oh, sure you have. The authors are a couple of—what do they call themselves?—cultural psychologists, or something. They've done three or four really

155

fascinating, best-selling books about different subcultures of American society. Real readable stuff. I think the last one was about a largely Hispanic town in Texas someplace. They don't do that usual visiting-researcher-questionnaire kind of thing. They just move in the neighborhood as ordinary people and learn about their neighbors."

Jane nodded. "I see. It makes sense. Come sit down and study the book, Shelley."

"Why? You want me to read the whole thing right now?"

"No, I just want you to look at it thoroughly."

"Is this some kind of game? You must be really bored."

"Indulge me."

Shelley sat down and read the material on the front flap, skimmed the chapter headings, read the back cover flap, then turned the book over. She set it down on the table. "Okay, so I've looked it over and I still don't get wha—"

She frowned for a moment, picked the book back up and turned it over. She studied the picture of the authors for a long moment. Then she looked up at Jane. Her jaw dropped and her eyes opened very wide. "Jane—?"

"Uh-huh?"

"This picture," Shelley said haltingly. "You'll think I'm crazy, but it looks like a glamour shot of Billy Joe and Tiffany."

Seventeen

"That's what *I* thought," Jane said.

"How'd you get this book?" Shelley asked.

"It came to our house by accident. An entire box of them. The mail carrier had a bunch of boxes from my parents and unloaded this one on us too. The kids didn't read the address label and ripped into it."

They hunched over the book, studying the picture closely. "Their hair is different. Both of them. And they're 'dressed for success' in the picture," Jane said. "But I'm sure they're the same people. They have the same teeth as the Johnsons do. I always notice teeth. It's stretching coincidence too far that they'd have exact doubles who just happened to send them a box full of books."

Shelley sat back, scowling. "So we're their next guinea pigs, right? They're doing this hillbilly act to shock the suburbanites and madly scribble down our reactions. That pisses me off."

"It hurts my feelings," Jane admitted. "I was going out of my way to like them, be nice to them, even defend them against the Concerned Citizen junk, and all the time they're considering me a lab rat. If their other books were such best-sellers, that means they're rich, probably highly sophisticated academics who are slumming."

"Right," Shelley said. "Wait while I get dressed."

"You're getting dressed to go to bed when you're already in your nightgown?"

"No, we're going to take that box of books to the rightful recipients."

The box was on the porch between them. Jane rang the bell and Tiffany opened the door. "Tiff, the post office accidentally gave me a package that belongs to you," Jane said. "I'm sorry to say my kids thought it was more Christmas packages from their grandparents and opened it."

She bent down and picked up one end of the box and Shelley got the other, although it didn't require two of them to carry it. The point was to get in the house without handing the box over to Tiffany—or Dr. Lenore Johnson, to be more accurate.

Tiffany looked alarmed. "Here you go, I'll take it," she said.

"No, no, we'll put it inside," Shelley said, coming very close to physically shoving Tiffany aside.

As arranged, Jane managed to trip going in the house and dropped her end of the box, which allowed a couple books to spill out.

"Oh, dear, I'm so sorry," she said, almost bumping heads with Tiffany as they both leaned over very quickly to pick up books.

Jane grabbed one while Tiffany frantically stuffed the others back.

"Hmmm," Jane said, holding it up. "What an interesting-looking subject." She flipped it over. "And what attractive authors. Somehow I have the feeling they're familiar."

She looked straight into Tiffany's eyes and tossed the book into the box.

Billy Joe had heard them talking and had come into the room. He was now standing behind Tiffany, who turned and looked at him panic-stricken, then back at Jane.

"You know, don't you?" she asked.

Jane nodded.

"And you're angry," Billy Joe said. It wasn't a question.

"We sure are," Shelley said.

It was amazing the way his very appearance changed when he dropped the twangy speech and good ol' boy grin. Even wearing overalls and a plaid shirt, he looked like a college professor now.

"I guess we should explain . . ." Billy Joe (Dr. William Johnson in the picture) said.

But Jane and Shelley weren't having any. "It's late. We have to go," Shelley said.

"Please—" Tiffany began.

"Nothing you can explain is going to improve our dispositions," Jane said. "I can promise you that."

Both of the Drs. Johnson were still sputtering fitfully as Jane and Shelley left the house. "Can you come in for a while?" Jane asked. "Or are you still planning to go to bed early?"

"I'm much too mad to sleep," Shelley said.

They tidied up the mess the kids had made with

dinner, fixed themselves soft drinks, and settled in Jane's living room. Jane dredged up a pack of cigarettes and lit one. It didn't help at all.

Shelley said, "When I read those other books they wrote, I really thought they were fascinating. But the idea of you and me and our families and neighbors being put under their sociological microscope makes me furious. I know that's selfish, not caring about other people's privacy, only my own. And being made to feel bad about myself makes me even angrier."

"Do they use people's real names?" Jane asked.

Shelley shrugged. "I hope not, but I don't know. The people they write about are very vivid. They probably fictionalize a bit and have to use fake names."

"But when the book about us comes out, we'll all be recognizable to each other, won't we," Jane said. "I'm just sick about this. It's a betrayal. A huge, mean-spirited practical joke."

Shelley nodded. "More to you than most of us, Jane. You went out of your way to be nice to them. I was only nice to them because I knew you'd take me to task if I weren't. This sure explains a lot, doesn't it?"

"What do you mean?"

"About them," Shelley said. "Why they seem too young to be retired. Why Billy Joe works at a computer and has lots of reference books. Why they appear to have plenty of money from an unknown source. Why they're renting instead of buying."

"Didn't Sharon Wilhite say she owns the house? Didn't she have to know they were fakes?"

"She probably rents it through an agency. I can't quite see her rushing home from the office to chat with potential renters. As for a signature on a contract, 'Billy Joe' really is William J. Johnson and Tiffany/Lenore probably didn't sign it."

Katie came thumping down the stairs, into the kitchen, and called out, "Thanks, Mom. I was gonna clean it all up. Really, I was."

"It's okay," Jane said listlessly.

Katie came in and looked at her mother, then reached out and pretended to take her pulse. "Are you okay? You should be mad at us."

"I'm too busy being mad at someone else just now."

"Oh, good," Katie said. "Does that mean you wouldn't care if I had a few girls over for the night?"

"It does not."

"Too bad," Katie said cheerfully and headed back to her room.

"It's Saturday night and none of my children asked to go anywhere!" Jane said, suddenly aware of something other than the Johnsons. "What's wrong with this picture?"

But Shelley wasn't willing to wander off the path. She was annoyed and she intended to stay annoyed until she'd hashed the whole situation out. "The strange thing is, they're changing their technique."

"What?"

"Well, I've only read two of the books. I think there are four. But in those two, the Johnsons moved into an area and tried to fit in. I remember something about learning to speak Spanish before moving into the Hispanic town and dying their hair dark so they'd fit in better. And in the one about the Pennsylvania mining community, they did a full year's research on the area, the history, the family names, mining terms, and such."

"But they didn't do that here," Jane mused.

"No, they set out to be as obvious and misplaced as possible," Shelley agreed.

"I wonder why."

"So do I. Maybe it's a marketing thing. Like, you know, the editor says the sales of the last book weren't as fabulous as the one before and they better jazz the new one up a bit."

"More of an exposé than a study, you mean. 'Look at how nasty these snobs are to somebody who doesn't fit in'?"

Shelley nodded. "Something like that, maybe. Skewering the subject group instead of merely describing them. Come to think of it, when I read the two books, as much as I enjoyed them for an insight into another subculture, I had a faintly uneasy sense that the people they studied were being patronized. Not quite skewered, just a hint. There were a lot of 'bad guys' and not many 'good guys.'"

"And housewives like us make excellent targets. Oh, Shelley, imagine how they might be describing my parties, or Suzie's blatant manhunting or Julie Newton's general ditsiness."

"Do you think they told the police the truth about

who they really are and what they're doing here?" Shelley asked. "They couldn't make up a story about their background in Hog Wallow or wherever they might claim to be from without a background check showing that they were lying. And lying to the police isn't a good idea."

Jane got up to refill their drinks. Shelley trailed along and opened the freezer door to get more ice. "Why don't you get that ice-maker fixed?"

"Inertia," Jane said.

"Got anything to eat?"

Jane laughed. "I'm the Queen of Leftover Cookies, Shelley."

As they sat back down to nibble, Jane said, "I wish Mel had more time to fill us in. Do you think I should call him?"

"And risk having to talk to Addie?"

"Good point. Shelley, could this mean they had something to do with Lance King's death? A motive? You used the word 'exposé' a while ago. If we're right about them changing their technique, they and Lance were both in the exposé business. Maybe he found out who they really were."

Shelley considered this. "But the worst he could have said about them was that they were best-selling authors. That's an accolade, not something to be ashamed of."

"If you're concealing the fact of how you earn your living—and it's a good living, it sounds like—having it known could be a big financial threat."

"Oh, right. We'd all be on our best behavior if we knew what they were really doing and they wouldn't get a true picture? Still, Jane, it doesn't seem to me to be a good enough motive to actually murder someone to keep them quiet. That would really wreck their careers if they were found out."

Jane lit another cigarette, wondering as she did whether two of them so close together would make her dizzy.

"I sincerely hope you're right, Shelley, because if knowing their true identity caused them to kill Lance King, you and I could be in big trouble. Now we know who they are."

Eighteen

Sunday morning Jane dragged herself and the kids to the nine o'clock church services. She didn't feel like getting dressed up and going out in the cold any more than they did. But then she often didn't feel like going and was always glad afterwards that she'd made the effort. The Sunday before Christmas was always especially beautiful and uplifting. It was really a lovely morning. Very cold and clear and very little wind and a brilliant sun shining on the two inches or so of new snow that had fallen overnight.

"See? That wasn't so bad, was it?" she said as they drove home.

Mike had the Sunday paper in the car and just rattled

it in reply. Todd was trying to get the comics away from his older brother and said nothing, but Katie said, "It was okay."

"Okay? Come on! I saw you going all gooey when those little bitty kids came up the aisle to put their gifts at the manger scene."

"All right. It was nice," Katie admitted. "They sure were cute, weren't they? Are the packages real presents?"

"Were you paying attention? They're presents for the children at the homeless shelter. Katie, see if the car heater's working right. It's awfully cold."

"The bank clock across the street showed it dropped four degrees while we were in church," Mike contributed from the back seat.

"I haven't had time to watch the news," Jane said. "Is it supposed to get really cold?"

There was a consensus of shrugs. Jane told herself to remember to leave the faucet dripping in the guest bathroom where the pipes were most likely to freeze. When they drove up to the house, Pet was at the side kitchen door and Mel was sitting in front keeping warm in his MG.

When they were all inside and had shed their coats, Jane started working on throwing together a real breakfast. "Mel, I thought I might make a nice big batch of chili for dinner. Would you and your mother like to come?"

"Can't," he said. "She's got some old friends who already invited us to dinner. I'd much rather come here. These are people I haven't seen since I was seven and have never missed."

He'd pitched in to help, handing her a carton of eggs from the fridge and getting out the butter to warm up in the microwave. Mike was already cooking the bacon, a job Jane despised, and Katie was lining up the bread for the toaster. Todd and Pet were at the table where he was doling out the comics to her, page by page.

"See, kids?" Jane warned. "You are your mother's children all your life. She just wants to show you off, Mel."

The doorbell rang and Jane automatically cracked another two eggs. Whoever it was would certainly want to eat.

"I lurked outside until I knew you were cooking," Ginger said. Pet helped her take her coat off. "Smells wonderful."

"You'll eat with us, won't you?" Jane asked.

"You think you could stop me? It's my least favorite meal to fix and most favorite to eat. Do you have cinnamon sugar? No? I'll fix some. It isn't breakfast without cinnamon sugar on butter-slathered toast."

Ginger made no effort to explain what she had come for and Jane began to wonder if she had just been cruising around looking for someone to feed her. Finally, as they were carrying plates to the dining room, since there was too much of a crowd for the kitchen, Ginger said, "I didn't just come to mooch food. I'd like to interview you."

"Me?" Jane asked. "Why?"

"Because of the party and Lance's death."

"Nope," Jane said. "I'm sorry."

"I won't use your name."

"I don't even know as much about it as you probably do," Jane said.

Ginger suddenly looked startled, as if someone had pinched her. She turned to Mel, who was trying to get his cinnamon sugar on the bread instead of all over the table and himself. "I'll bet you didn't get anything off Lance's computer, right?"

"Nope," he said. "Nothing of any use."

"Oh, God! I feel so stupid and you're going to want to smack me—"

Mel put his toast down and looked at her. "Why?" he asked in a very ominous tone of voice.

"Well, I'd forgotten something. Lance told me once that he never, never worked directly on the hard drive. I thought he was just trying to discourage me from messing with his computer to see what kind of stories he was working on. But then I started noticing that every single time he used it, when he turned it off, he took out the disk and put it in his pocket."

"He didn't have a disk on him when he died," Mel said.

"Then he must have lost it somewhere, because he always had at least one, and usually a couple on him."

Mel said, "Jane, you didn't find a disk here, did you?"

"No, and I did a fairly good cleaning between the

caroling party and the cookie party. It's not something you could accidentally vacuum up."

"Then it's probably outside somewhere in the snow. Hell!" he said. With obvious regret and a meaningful glare at Ginger, he pushed his plate away, got up, and went to the phone. When he got back, he said, "I have some people coming over to search. As cold as it's getting, that's sure going to make me real popular."

"Then finish your breakfast while you're waiting," Jane insisted. "They won't be here instantly and if it's out there, it's been there a while already. Ten minutes more won't matter."

The yellow tape, which had been removed from the Johnsons' yard, was replaced. Mel and three other officers borrowed rakes from several neighbors and started scratching up all the new snow. Two other officers were precariously doing the same on the roof. Jane had generously offered to help, knowing full well they wouldn't let a "civilian" on the grounds. Nor was there any sign of Billy Joe and Tiffany.

Jane had wanted to talk to Mel about her brief conversation with them the night before and her and Shelley's discovery of who they really were, but there wasn't time to speak privately. Especially not with a reporter in the house. Nor could she mention the talk they'd had with Sharon Wilhite.

The police presence at the Johnson house again had drawn quite a crowd. Neighbors pretending to be out on walks stopped by and gawked. The influx of traffic that the holiday decorations had caused added to the confusion. A number of cars stopped and their occupants wandered over to the yellow tapes to ask what was going on. Other reporters from the newspapers and television stations turned up. Jane got out the monster coffeemaker, made up a strong, hot brew, and took cups of it over to Mel to distribute among his people.

The temperature continued to fall. Jane remembered the pipes and left a slow stream of water running in the guest bathroom. Shelley had called almost immediately when the police tape went up to see what was going on and came over about two to do a little gawking of her own from Jane's bedroom window. They lamented over the fact that Jane hadn't had an opportunity to tell Mel what they'd found out. Not that he didn't already know more than they did.

"Have you seen anything of the Johnsons?" Shelley asked.

"Not hide nor hair . . . nor costume," Jane said. "I presume they're in the house, but they haven't stepped foot outside that I've noticed since the police surrounded their house again."

As she spoke, she caught a glimpse of Billy Joe cutting across between their house and Jane's. "I think he's coming here, Shelley. Oops, you missed him."

"You're not going to let him in your house, are you?"

Jane thought for a second. "He's not simple-minded. I can't imagine he'd think he could walk through a whole flock of police, come in here and kill both of us, and walk back through the flock without raising suspicion."

"Okay, but I'll watch from up here," Shelley said. "If it looks like trouble, I'll open a window and scream the place down."

Jane let Billy Joe wait in the cold for a while and opened the door after he'd rung twice. "Yes?" she asked coolly.

He'd abandoned the Billy Joe persona and looked very "Ivy League on a Sunday Off." He was wearing a Harvard sweatshirt, jeans, expensive-looking hiking boots, and a parka like the one Jane had considered getting Mike for Christmas that had cost nearly as much as her first car. He really did look like a different person.

"May I come in for one minute? Just one minute."

"I suppose so."

Jane opened the door a little wider and stood aside, but didn't move from the hallway.

"Mrs. Jeffry, I want you to know that we're leaving as soon as we can make arrangements."

"Oh?" She tried, quite unsuccessfully, she was sure, to feign indifference.

"We didn't count on someone so clever being right next door. And we know you'll tell your neighbors."

"Naturally I will. Why should I keep your secret?" Then, thinking quickly, she added, "I already have, in fact. Quite a few of them."

"It was a bad idea from the beginning," he said.

170

"And I don't blame you for feeling you've been tricked. You're a good person. You were kind and thoughtful to the people you thought we were. And the more outrageous we got, the kinder you became."

Jane softened a little. But only a little. "So you're going to go try this somewhere else, I guess. Play your nasty little academic deception on others."

"I really am sorry."

Jane's manners fought with her feelings and lost. "You should be. Good-bye, Dr. Johnson."

He left without another word. Jane closed the door and looked up the stairs. "You heard all that?" she asked Shelley, who was already on her way down.

"I did. Do you believe him?"

"It didn't occur to me not to. You think that was just another act?"

"It seemed sincere," Shelley said. "But he seemed sincere when he was good ol' boy Billy Joe, too."

"I guess you're right."

"That was brilliant of you to say you'd told the neighbors about him."

"I thought it was pretty good, too," Jane said. "Kind of spreads the danger out, if they *are* dangerous. They might have done in Lance King if he was going to wreck their finances by ruining their next book deal. It's a real stretch to imagine they could bump both of us off, and they're too smart to think they could kill off the whole neighborhood."

Shelley grinned. "Counterproductive anyway. It would leave them no one to study."

The phone rang and Jane was still chuckling as she picked it up.

"Mrs. Jeffry? This is Sam Dwyer. Do you have a minute? I wanted to thank you for inviting me to your party yesterday and wondered if I could return the favor?"

"How nice, but there's no need. I was glad you could come. Your fudge was terrific, too."

"Pet and I would like to invite your family to dinner tonight. She told me you'd mentioned making chili and I make a terrific pot of chili. Bring all your kids, if you like."

"How nice of you. My older son has a date tonight, but I'll see about the others and get back to you."

"No need. I'll make enough for everyone and Pet and I will eat the leftovers. Is five-thirty too early?"

"Well, that sounded chummy," Shelley said when Jane had hung up.

"It was Sam Dwyer inviting me and the kids to dinner," Jane said. "Nice break from cooking for me."

"A date with Sam Dwyer," Shelley mused.

"Date! Shelley, bite your tongue. It isn't a date!"

"Sounds like one to me."

Jane shook her head. "No, nobody invites you to bring three kids on a date."

"I think Sam's got the hots for you."

Jane blushed. "Don't be goofy. He must have just decided it's time to get to know some of his neighbors and he started with us because I had the cookie party."

"No, it's more than that. I couldn't get him to talk to

me at all and Suzie struck out, too. I think he likes you. A nice widow for the nice widower."

"Wrong, wrong, wrong!"

But when Shelley had gone, she found herself thinking, *Do I have a date with Sam Dwyer? I don't believe Mel's going to like that much.*

Nineteen

Katie and Mike had other plans for dinner, or at least Katie claimed she did, but Jane insisted that Todd come along with her to the Dwyers'. If she didn't take along at least one child, she was afraid the dinner would qualify as A Date, notwithstanding Pet's presence. Shelley's joking about it had struck Jane seriously. Was Sam Dwyer interested in her? Shelley had raised a valid point. He'd been unwilling to talk to anyone else, but came to a party at her house and engaged her in pleasant conversation. Was he undergoing some change, thinking he needed a social life for Pet's sake, or had he really found Jane interesting?

If so, she'd have to nip it in the bud. She liked her life just like it was, with Mel a big part of it. But as she watched the police searching the yard next door from her bedroom window, her thoughts wandered into dangerous territory. Sam Dwyer seemed like a nice enough guy. What if he turned out to be nicer and more interesting than she knew? What if she found herself attracted to him?

No, don't consider it, she told herself. She was just being neurotic. "Borrowing trouble" as her mother would have put it.

The sky had grown overcast again and it was starting to get dark already by four. The police were stopping work for the day, returning lawn rakes, shaking their heads in irritation.

"You didn't find the disk?" Jane asked, when Mel came to the door.

"No, and I don't think it's there. Any coffee left?"

Jane poured him a big cup and sat down with him at the kitchen table. "I've got to talk fast, Mel. The kids and I are invited out to an early dinner at a neighbor's, but there were a couple things I wanted to run by you." Well, the kids were all invited, and Sam Dwyer was a neighbor, so it wasn't a lie.

"Been snooping?"

"Just keeping our eyes and ears open," she said huffily. "I presume you know that Sharon Wilhite is Lance King's ex-wife?"

"She told us that."

Jane quickly ran through the high points of what Sharon had told her and Shelley. "Does that match what she told you?"

"As if scripted," he said wryly.

"Does that mean you don't believe her?"

"Not necessarily. But I'm having a little trouble figuring out why she'd come to your house when there was the least chance he'd be here. If I were she, I'd have avoided it like the plague."

174

"Did you ask her that?" Jane said.

Mel nodded. "She said she'd heard he was coming, then heard he wasn't, so she figured there was no danger of running into him. Maybe she trusts in gossip more than I do."

"She doesn't strike me as a Pollyanna type," Jane said. She glanced at her watch. She needed to move this conversation along so that she didn't have to discuss just which neighbor had invited her to dinner. "The other thing Shelley and I learned was about the Johnsons."

He said, "I can't tell you anything about them."

"Yes, but I can. They're sociologists or 'cultural historians' or something. They faked the hillbilly act to spy on the neighborhood for a new book they're writing."

Mel nodded.

"You knew? And you weren't going to tell me?"

"Not until King's murder is sorted out. I should have known you'd pry it out of them yourself."

"I didn't pry it out of them. It fell in my lap. Or rather, my front hall. A box of copies of their newest book was delivered here and the kids opened it by mistake. I saw the picture of them on the back."

Mel's eyes widened. "Why doesn't information find its way to me so easily?"

"Do you suspect them?"

"Because they were faking an identity? Nope. They told us right away who they really were and what they were up to. It was, marginally, a legitimate deception.

Nothing illegal about it, at least."

Jane glanced at her watch. Quarter of five. And she still had to change her clothes and put on fresh makeup. "How's your mother getting along?"

"Mom! Dinner! Hell!" he said, suddenly getting up. "I've got to go, Jane. I'll give you a call later. Or drop by if I can."

As he was struggling into his coat, Jane asked, "Are you making progress with this investigation?"

He hesitated for a minute. "Nope," he said with discouraged honesty. "Don't take that to mean, however, that you and Shelley need to interfere."

"There's that word again," Jane said with a smile. "We don't 'interfere.' We just sometimes provide you with a more domestic view of things."

"Yeah, right," Mel said, giving her a perfunctory kiss and plunging out into the cold.

Sam Dwyer had done a good job of being both father and mother, at least as far as the appearance of the house went. It wasn't high style, but it was cozy and homey, with a lot of the niceties that men don't often notice. There were lots of afghans tossed around on the furniture, throw pillows, pictures on the walls. The Christmas tree was huge and decorated almost entirely with things Pet had made or taken a fancy to. There were lots of little dolls, ornaments with globs of glitter, and unidentifiable stuff that had been made with love, if not artistic ability.

Pet immediately took Todd off to see yet another

new computer game she'd gotten. Jane followed the smell of chili to the kitchen. Sam turned and said, "Sorry I didn't meet you at the door. I was cutting up some extra onions. Sit down. Make yourself at home, Jane."

Jane glanced around the kitchen. It was larger than that of most of the unrenovated houses in the neighborhood. Maybe that's why Sam had chosen it. Judging from the smell of the chili and the expert way he was dicing onions, he was a serious cook. There was a rack of expensive cooking pans of every size hanging above the sink and on the windowsill there was a row of tiny pots full of growing herbs in miniature wooden crates.

"I'm told my chili is only one chemical reaction away from lava," he said, "but I've tried to keep the spice to a minimum this time."

"It smells wonderful. You must be a good cook."

"My wife didn't like to cook and she was awful at it, so I had to learn. Took some classes and discovered I was a fair hand at it. Would you like a drink? I have iced tea, sangria, coffee . . . ?"

"Sangria would go well with chili, thanks."

"I think so, too." He poured two glasses after washing his hands thoroughly to get rid of the onion odor, and sat down across from her. "Do you cook?" he asked.

Jane almost laughed at the bluntness of the question. "I do. We'd starve otherwise. Actually, I cook a few things very, very well. But it's the day-in-and-day-out, just-for-nourishment cooking that drives me crazy."

"We ought to consider trading off dinners," he said. "Save each of us half the trouble."

"Maybe so," Jane said uneasily.

"Are you from this area?" he asked.

"No, I'm not from anywhere really," Jane said. She explained briefly that her father was in the State Department and owing to his downright spooky gift for picking up almost any language in a matter of days, she and her sister Marty had spent most of their childhood either traveling with their parents, or stuck in the nearest boarding school. "He'd be what they used to call an 'idiot savant' except that he isn't an idiot," Jane said.

"But you've lived here quite a while, haven't you?"

"Oh, yes. My childhood was interesting, but I wouldn't wish it on anyone. When I married, I was determined to raise my kids in the same house for all their growing-up years. Fortunately, I married a man who had rock-deep family ties here, so there was never any danger of having to move."

"I thought you were a widow. Someone told me that."

"I am. But I've stuck in place anyway." She was a bit wary about being questioned and certainly had no intention of getting all chummy and telling him about her finances and how she managed to keep the house, unlike many divorced or widowed women did.

Sam topped up her sangria and looked like he was about to ask her something else.

"And what about you?" she said quickly.

"Oh, much the same, I think. My dad was closer to the idiot side and could never keep a job. But the result was the same. Lots of moving, no sense of home. Not much sense of family either. Lots of times he'd have to work quite a while in a new job before he could send for us and in the meantime my mom had to work to make ends meet. I feel like you do about raising children in the same place."

"How long have you been here?"

"Only a few years. Since Pet's mother died. But it's where we're staying. And I'm lucky enough to have a job that lets me stay home and be available to her whenever she needs me."

"You speak of your wife's death very calmly," Jane said.

"And so do you of your husband's," he pointed out.

"That's true. But at the end, it wasn't a happy marriage," she said. One of the great understatements. Steve had been leaving her for another woman on an icy February night when his car hit a guardrail.

"Neither was mine," he admitted. "I've got to check the cornbread."

"Can I do anything to help?" Jane asked.

"You could. I'm afraid I left the newspaper all over the dining room table. If you could just stuff it in the recycling bin in that closet."

Jane liked it when people accepted an offer to help as sincere. Besides, in this case it was a good way to put an end to what might be polite inquiry on his part, but was seeming more like a job interview.

She gathered up the newspaper and opened the closet door. It was more of a pantry, really, with long shelves along one wall and recycling bins tucked under them. Sam Dwyer was, it appeared, seriously into recycling. In the paper bin there were not only newspapers, but cardboard egg cartons, leftover wrapping paper, magazines, a couple of flattened boxes. The metal bin was the same way. Not only soda and food cans, but even wads of used aluminum foil. This was a seriously over-organized person. Well, what could you expect from a man who actually wore an apron to cook? A masculine apron, but still . . . an apron.

Smiling to herself, she realized she was in absolutely no danger of falling for him.

This allowed her to enjoy her evening. The chili was spicy, but good, with lovely bits of real tomatoes in the sauce and a hint of some mysterious flavor she couldn't quite pin down, but suspected was just a breath of nutmeg. Sam had also made cornbread with a green chili sauce and a lot of paprika in the mix that was fabulous. There were deviled eggs, crisp celery stalks with a cream cheese stuffing, and tiny crackers that looked a bit like spaetzle that had been boiled then baked. Sam preened about them. They were his own culinary invention, but he didn't reveal the secret of making them. Just as well, Jane thought, she'd probably make a botch of it.

The kids ignored the subtlety of the food and just

wolfed it down as if they were starving. Todd had a soft drink with his dinner; Pet had her special milk poured from a lovely old-fashioned pitcher. Jane was astonished that Pet, who appeared rather fragile, managed to outeat Todd. How nice for Sam that he hadn't gotten a picky eater for a child.

As soon as they finished eating, the kids went back to their computer game, which Jane regretted. This was supposed to be a family gathering and it would have been nice if the family members had all stuck it out.

Sam wasn't in any hurry to clear the table and get on with dessert. After Jane had finished her effusive and heartfelt compliments on the meal, he went into questioning mode again. But this time, it was about Lance King, not Jane. This amused her. He, more than anyone else in the neighborhood, had seemed disinterested in it. He hadn't, to her knowledge, walked up the block to ask the neighbors what was going on, which was what nearly everyone else had done.

"What were the police doing this afternoon with rakes in the middle of winter?" he asked.

Jane figured enough people knew the answer that she wouldn't be giving away anything she shouldn't. "Apparently Lance King kept notes about people he might go after on a computer disk, rather than on the computer itself. At least, that's what his assistant, Ginger, says. They haven't found the disk and seem to think it may have fallen out of his pocket either while he was climbing onto the roof or when he went off the edge."

"What a strange thing to do. Disks are fragile. Do they suspect someone of taking it?"

"I have absolutely no idea what the police think of anything," Jane said firmly. "And to be truthful, I'm tired of the whole thing. What with the usual stress of Christmas and the neighbors who put up decorations that have drawn half of Chicago to stare at their house, Lance King's murder is just too much to cope with."

He got the hint and didn't ask anything more. Instead, he turned on the radio to a classical station and started cleaning up the table. "I guess I'd feel the same way if I were closer to it all," he said. "But it'll soon be over. The holidays and the investigation."

"Or maybe not," Jane said. "There are murders that are never solved. I'm not entirely sure this might not be one of them."

Twenty

Sam made a couple of trips with dishes, this time turning down Jane's offer to assist. While he was on the first trip, she took a sip of the milk substitute Pet had left in her glass. Good stuff. Tasted just like the real thing, but probably cost the earth. Thank heavens none of her own kids had allergies that demanded substitute foods. What a nuisance.

Sam called Todd and Pet back to the table and

brought out dessert, which was cut-up flour tortillas, deep-fried and dusted with sugar. They helped settle the chili, he claimed. But the chili was giving Jane a bit of stomach trouble, which she hated because she'd always prided herself on having a cast-iron digestive tract.

When they finished dessert, Jane said, "That was a superb dinner, Sam," in a tone she hoped suggested finality.

"You're not leaving, are you?"

"I hate to be rude, but I do have to get back home. I still have tons to do today. I'm not even through wrapping Christmas presents."

"Oh," Pet said. "I wanted to show you my scrapbook with pictures of my mom."

"Pet, I'm sure Mrs. Jeffry can come back and see them some other time," Sam said.

But Pet looked so disappointed that Jane had to relent. "Presents can wait a little while, I guess. I'd love to see your pictures."

While Sam cleaned up dinner, Pet got out her scrapbook which was in a protective cover. She sat down next to Jane on the sofa and presented it proudly. It was well-worn. Apparently Pet had a deep sense of loss for the mother she couldn't remember. Jane wondered if Sam had given any thought to a little therapy for the child. It couldn't be easy for him, either, being as he'd said the marriage wasn't a real good one.

The first picture was a wedding shot. Stiff, formal. Or at least the much younger Sam was standing rigid with a frozen smile. The bride, however, looked like she was having the time of her life. The photographer had caught her in what looked like the middle of a laugh. She wasn't really beautiful, except in the way all brides are automatically beautiful, but she looked high-spirited and happy. Medium-brown hair like Pet's, but lots of it, all fluffed out and curling all over the place. The gown was cut a bit low and there was an expanse of bulging bosom that wasn't quite virginal.

"Your mother was very pretty, Pet," Jane said. Pet nodded solemnly.

The next pictures were badly done snapshots. The newlywed couple posed by a presumably new car with palm trees in the background. Sitting on a beach and all but invisible under a big umbrella. Playing with a dog in a tiny fenced yard. In every picture, Pet's mom was laughing and Sam was looking serious. No wonder they hadn't gotten along. There was just the slightest suggestion of "the floozy with a heart of gold" in Pet's mom's appearance. Not trashy, just a little more voluptuous and carefree than most women. But then, she was young, too.

"This is my favorite," Pet said, turning to a new page.

It was her mother in a maternity dress, standing sideways with a great, bulging midsection.

"That's me," Pet said with a giggle. It was the first time Jane had heard Pet sound genuinely happy. "That was the night before I was born."

"That's a great picture. I have one like that, too. The day before Mike was born. What was your mother's name, Pet?"

"Patricia. Like me. Only she was called Patty Sue."

The rest of the pictures told a story that Pet probably wouldn't understand until she was older. The pictures of Patty Sue with Pet, and there were a lot of them, were the old Patty Sue, laughing and happy. Those with Sam and Patty Sue alone were serious. A filmed history of a marriage falling apart. Someday Jane might have to look through her photos and see if her own marriage had gone to pieces in the photo record.

Or maybe she wouldn't.

The last picture was of Pet's third birthday. She was sitting on Patty Sue's lap with a birthday cake in front of them and icing all over Pet's face. Patty Sue was wiping away tears of laughter. Sam wasn't in the picture.

"Pet, your scrapbook is wonderful. You're so lucky to have all these pictures and I'm sure you'll treasure them all your life," Jane said.

"Thank you, Mrs. Jeffry," Pet said, closing the album and putting it in a plastic bag that protected it. Just then Todd, still playing at the computer in the den, called to her and she excused herself quite properly and left the room.

Too bad Pet hadn't gotten to have her mother a little longer, Jane thought. She might have absorbed more of the woman's sense of fun and frivolity. Pet *did* need to be tickled sometimes and Jane guessed that Patty

Sue had been a tickling kind of mother.

"Sam, I have to get home," she said, going into the kitchen. "I'm worried about my water pipes. The wind's picked up and that'll make the cold worse."

"I'll drive you home," he said, closing the door on the dishwasher. The kitchen was spotless.

"No, it's only three houses away. No use you going out, too."

Luckily, the mild fight to get Todd away from the computer game and into his outerwear prevented any extended good-byes or anything more specific than Sam's vague remark about doing this again someday. Todd raced away up the street, while Jane followed as quickly as she could without risking a fall.

As she came in the kitchen door, Todd greeted her with a grim face. "Mom, old thing, you're not going to like this."

"Not the pipes!"

He nodded. "I went in the guest bathroom and heard a noise in the basement. Water everywhere."

"Perfect! Just perfect! Sunday night with broken pipes!"

"Go ahead, Mom. Say 'shit.'"

"Shit!"

It didn't help. But it made Todd yelp with laughter.

"Mrs. Pargeter, may I speak with Bruce."

After a short pause, Bruce answered.

"Bruce, it's Jane Jeffry. I hate myself for asking this—I really know all about keeping pipes from freezing and I left the water running, but Katie didn't know and turned it off and what I don't know is where the little handle to turn the flow off is. I've been slogging around in the basement—" She could hear her voice rising to an hysterical squeak but couldn't help it.

"I'll find the shut-off valve for you," Bruce said calmly. "Can't fix the pipe tonight though."

"But we'll have other water, right?"

"Maybe. I'll have to see the system."

Jane stomped around, looking for another flashlight as hers was already going dim and she was afraid to turn on the basement light. Water and electricity didn't go together well, she'd heard. Bruce arrived quickly and seemed quite confident that it was no big deal, even though he hadn't looked over the situation yet.

"Why's it dark down here?" he asked at the head of the basement stairs. Jane started to explain her understanding of electricity, but Bruce laughed, flipped on the basement light and went down the steps. He was back in less than five minutes.

"You're lucky. That guest bath is an addition to the original plan and has its own shut-off valve. I'll get back in the morning and fix it."

"I have water everywhere else? What a relief! Oh, Bruce, I'm so thankful."

He brushed off her thanks. "I finished up Mrs. Newton's kitchen today and nobody usually wants anything done over the holidays except emergencies like this. Glad to do it. See you tomorrow."

Weak with relief, Jane went to the comfort of her favorite squashy chair in the living room and collapsed. It was horrible to contemplate how much worse it might have been. A houseful of kids, last-minute holiday activities, and no water! Yikes!

It was Sunday night and she deserved to veg out. She wondered what was on *Masterpiece Theatre*. It was a measure of how hectic life had been the last couple days that she couldn't remember. She hoped it was something very soothing. A Jane Austen movie, maybe. She glanced at her watch and was surprised that it was only six-thirty. She looked around for the television controller, loathe to get up again even to turn the set on. Not on the coffee table. Not at the side of the chair. She leaned forward and fished around underneath the front of the chair, then remembered that the last time she'd lost it, it was down in the plump cushions. Ah, there it was.

No, it wasn't. The hard plastic object she pulled out was a computer disk.

The missing disk? It wasn't one of hers. She only bought the brightly colored ones. This one was black. And unlabeled.

She hoisted herself out of the chair with effort and dialed Mel's number to leave a message. She was surprised that he answered. "Didn't you go out to dinner with your mother?" she asked, momentarily distracted from her purpose.

"I begged off and I'm in deep trouble. But I was cold clear through and would have died soon if I hadn't soaked in a hot bath. What's up?"

Jane reported what she'd found.

"Is it the one we're looking for?" he asked.

"I imagine so. It's not one of mine. And it's not a game disk. There's no label."

"I'll be right over," he said with a martyred sigh.

Jane hung up, stood for a moment in thought, and went down to boot up her computer.

Twenty-one

Before Mel could pull himself together and get over to pick up the disk, Jane's doorbell rang. It was Ginger, all bundled up and looking perky.

"I'm here for our interview," she said.

Jane didn't invite her in. "Ginger, I'm not doing an interview. Period. I told you that."

"But I thought—"

"No, I made it very clear the first time you asked. You couldn't have misunderstood. And I'm really sorry, but I can't invite you in. I'm busy."

Ginger looked surprised, but not offended. "Well, you win some, you lose some. Did the police find the disk?"

"No, they didn't," Jane said truthfully. She was glad Ginger hadn't phrased the question "Has the disk been found?"

"Okay," Ginger agreed a little too readily. "I'll work on another angle."

Jane shut the door on her and watched through the little window in it as Ginger headed for her car. Mel turned into the driveway just then and Ginger changed course. Apparently she was questioning him and he was making "no comment" gestures. She accepted this rejection as well in apparent good spirits.

Jane was standing at the door with the disk in hand when he reached her.

"You're sure this is the right one?" he asked.

"No, I'm just sure it's not mine. And it was in the chair he flung himself into the night he was here."

Mel looked miserably cold and tired as he trudged back to his car with the disk in his pocket.

Jane raced for the phone. "Shelley! I found the disk. It was in my favorite chair in the living room. Down in the cushions."

"Have you called Mel?"

"He just picked it up."

"Oh," Shelley said with disappointment. "I was hoping we could take a quick look at it before you turned it over."

"We can. I made a copy of it."

"Jane! You're brilliant!"

Shelley arrived seconds later, looking uncharacteristically disheveled. "Pop it in your computer. Let's see what's on it."

They headed for the basement.

"What's the water over by the laundry room door?" Shelley asked.

"Broken pipe," Jane said. Half an hour ago this was

a crisis; now she was hardly interested enough to answer the question.

Jane punched a few keys and produced a list of the files on the disk. "Oh, good, he's saved these in the same word processing program that I have. That'll make it easier." She punched a few more keys and sat back smugly while the computer clicked and hummed. Then a screen she'd never seen before came up.

PASSWORD: _____

"Password?" they said in one voice.

"Hell!" Shelley added for good measure.

Jane typed in: LANCE.

The screen said: ACCESS DENIED—INVALID PASSWORD.

"Try 'King,'" Shelley said.

That didn't work either. Neither did 'Lanceking' or the call letters of the television station.

"This is hopeless," Shelley said. "There are about a million words and a lot more that aren't even real words that he could have used."

"No, people usually use something that's easy to remember so they don't lock themselves out of their own stuff. I wonder if he's listed in the phone book."

Shelley grabbed one from the shelf. "How surprising. Yes, he is. Or somebody with the same name." Shelley gave her the street address, which didn't work, and the telephone number, which didn't work either.

"Bring a pad of paper and a pencil upstairs while I

make coffee," Jane said. "Let's write a list of things to try."

They ended up with a long string of words: reporter, television, Wilhite, research, dossiers, jerk ("No, we think of him that way, he probably didn't," Shelley said), and a couple dozen others. Coffee'd up, they went back down and tried them all out. None worked.

"Okay," Jane said, closing her eyes as if to summon up a vision. "We have to pretend that we are Lance King—"

"Yuck."

"He'd use a word he likes," Jane said. She opened her eyes and tapped in the word "scandal."

It didn't work. Shelley said, "No, we have to really think like he did. He didn't see his work as scandal-mongering. He saw himself as the guardian of the public."

Jane typed in "guardian."

The computer said: PASSWORD ACCEPTED. PROCEED.

They shrieked.

Jane studied the list of files. They were numbered. She picked 001. It opened up and they groaned.

The text was in code. Not a computer code, just an ordinary code.

File 001 said: *Kamoieppi Pixvup—xet e tvoqqis op dummihi. Qsutvovoap vuu? Djidl vuxp sidusft gus vjuti ziest.*

"What now, Sherlock?" Shelley asked.

"I dunno. Do you suppose it's a simple letter substitution?"

"Maybe. If we dump them all together, alphabetize, and count each letter, we should be able to figure out which one represents E. It's the most common."

"Big help. We'd know one letter," Jane said. "Maybe it's a foreign language. It does look like a language, doesn't it. I could ask Mel if Lance was fluent in something or other."

"And you don't think he'd wonder just a bit why you're asking? I presume you didn't mention having copied this disk."

"You've got a point. My dad! My dad knows languages!"

"Can you E-mail him?"

"Yes, I'll do that. Let me print this one out. They're in the Netherlands. Heaven knows what time of day or night it is there now."

"Probably about two in the morning," Shelley said.

"I'll do that right after we print all the files out. You know, I do those letter substitution things in the puzzle magazines sometimes. If that's what this is, it shouldn't be that hard to do."

Shelley was doubtful. "But Jane, those give you clues. Like all the words in the list have to do with carnivals or something. And when they're sentences, they're real sentences with lots of 'the's and 'for's and such. This is just the man's personal notes. They're probably just phrases."

"It can't hurt to try anyway."

Jane made duplicate copies of each of the small files on paper, one set for her, one for Shelley, and sent an E-mail to her father before they abandoned the cold and rather damp-smelling basement.

"My family will think I've run away from home," Shelley said. "I can't remember if I even mentioned I was coming over here, I was in such a rush. I'll work on this at home and give you a call if I figure anything out."

Jane dinked around with the printouts for nearly an hour and got nowhere. It was no wonder, considering what a long day it had been, that she felt brain-dead. It was still Sunday, the day that had started out with church. But that morning seemed like it was days and days ago. She'd put the coded messages away somewhere safe and let her subconscious work on them while she was busy with other things. She got another sheet of paper and started making yet another list of reminders to herself.

The day after tomorrow was Christmas Eve day. Her shopping was done, but a lot of wrapping remained. Note: Get more tape and ribbon.

Christmas Eve day was also the normal trash pickup day. Would they send the monster trucks around on what was normally a half holiday? She hoped so. The parties she'd given had generated so much trash that if she didn't get it out this week, it would become a whole Dumpster load by the next week. Note: Put out trash and recycle.

That made her think about Sam Dwyer and his

fanatic recycling. She had a lot of plastic-coated paper plates. She'd just put them in a big bag. But if she were to recycle them, would they go in the plastics bin or the paper bin?

Her mind was going. No question about it. She remembered the "fortune" she'd made up at the Chinese restaurant—that her daughter would take care of her when she was old and dotty and wanted to wear her panties on her head. At the rate she was going, that might be next week.

She waited up, half watching television, half napping, playing (and losing) a few games of solitaire on her laptop until Katie and Mike had both come home. Then she went upstairs and took a long, soaky bath. When she got out, she was shocked to discover that it was only ten o'clock. It seemed like the middle of the night. Would this day never end?

While she was soaking, she'd thought of some other things that had to be done tomorrow and went back downstairs to fetch her list. Note: Call Marty. Her sister Marty was living in Tupelo this year. Unlike Jane, who had vowed not to move out of the neighborhood, let alone move around the world once she no longer had to, Marty and her husband couldn't stop moving. *"It's the only way I get my closets and drawers cleaned out,"* Marty told her.

Jane had long since given up putting Marty's addresses and phone numbers into her book in ink. Just pencil. But wherever Marty went, it was never Chicago. They hadn't laid eyes on each other for at least five years. Marty and her jerk of a husband also always seemed to find someone to impose themselves on at holidays, so Jane had to call her the day before to pass along her good wishes.

Note: Call Uncle Jim. He was a lifelong friend of her parents who had retired from the army and was a tough old Chicago cop now. Though he was no relation in blood, he was dear to her and she always had him over for holidays and any other time she could snag him. She needed to make sure he knew what time to come for Christmas dinner. Had she wrapped his present yet? She ran back downstairs to check. Yes, the big red foil package. It was a fine leather briefcase. He'd rumble about it, say she'd better start watching how she threw away her money, claim that if the punks on the street didn't steal it, the punks in his office would. But he'd treasure it anyway.

It was only 10:20. Jane was still too wound up from the long day to sleep. But if she got in bed and was ready to sleep, maybe it would creep up on her. She called to the cats, who insisted on sleeping in her bed, gathered up the coded messages, turned off the television and downstairs lights, and made her way slowly up the stairs, tripping over Max and Meow and dropping her pencil.

Mike had his stereo booming out something awful. She tapped on his door, opened it, and asked him to turn it down. "I have to drown out Willard," he said. The big dog was sound asleep in the middle of the floor, his snoring almost as loud as the music.

"Make sure you send him outside one more time before you go to bed," she said. "Unless you want a cleaning job in the morning."

Katie was, naturally, on the phone. Getting her a line of her own was among the smartest things Jane had ever done. Katie made a "wait, wait" gesture and ended her conversation. "Mom, I was just thinking, since you have to have the pipes fixed in that bathroom, why don't you redecorate it? It's kinda ratty-looking. We could go out and look at wallpaper and sinks and stuff after Christmas while I'm out of school."

"I think that's a great idea. I'll get a bid from Bruce Pargeter when he comes back tomorrow."

Todd was already asleep when she peeked in his room. How *could* he sleep through Mike's music!

She went to her own room and the cats made a beeline for the bed. The Johnsons had turned off their Christmas lights and music, so she could have her curtains open again. It had been disconcerting these last few days to wake up in a darkened room.

She pulled the curtains back and looked at the wreck of their backyard. The police had certainly churned up the snow with their rakes. As Jane's eyes adjusted to the relative darkness outside, she noticed that one space between the houses must have been raked clear down to the grass. There was a dark area.

She squinted her eyes. The dark area looked almost like a person.

Actually, the dark area looked *exactly* like a person.

She reached once more for the phone and dialed Mel's number.

Twenty-two

Jane woke at nine in a state of instant panic. Bruce Pargeter was coming over to work on the broken pipe. More important, Mel would certainly check in and she was desperately eager to hear what he'd have to say about the events of last night.

She'd been unable to get to sleep until almost four in the morning and now staggered out of bed, bleary and tired and pointedly avoiding looking out the bedroom or bathroom windows. She could hear voices downstairs. She showered and dressed hurriedly and threw on a bare minimum of makeup. Just enough that the bags under her eyes wouldn't actually frighten impressionable young children. Not that there were likely to be any around.

"Mom, Mel called while you were in the shower," Mike said when she came downstairs. "Said she was probably going to be okay. He's stopping by in a couple minutes."

Jane nodded and made her way to the coffeemaker. Thank God! Mike had started it for her. She poured a cup, added lots of cream and sugar, and gulped it down as quickly as she could. Ah . . . caffeine!

"What's that noise?" she asked Mike as she came closer to full consciousness.

"Bruce Pargeter. In the basement fixing things," Mike said.

Jane looked at Katie, who was excavating her cereal for raisins. "You can buy boxes of raisins, you know," Jane said. "All by themselves."

"But they aren't sugary or wet," Katie said. "What went on last night?"

"Somebody tried to bump off that reporter," Mike said. "The redheaded woman, Ginger."

"Why?" Katie asked.

Mike shrugged. Jane said, "We don't know."

"Maybe Mel does," Mike said. "Here he comes."

Katie, still in her robe and fuzzy slippers, went away to get dressed.

"You, too, Todd," Jane shouted into the living room where her youngest was cruising television channels. "No slobbing around in jammies."

Mel looked as exhausted as Jane felt. She wondered if men didn't sometimes wish they could use makeup to spruce themselves up a bit. "Ginger's okay?" she asked, as she slipped some bread into the toaster for him.

"Not okay. But she'll make it," he said. "She's suffered frostbite, a concussion, and has a broken wrist. She only regained consciousness about an hour ago."

"Did you get to talk to her?"

"Yes, but she wasn't making much sense. Had no idea what she was doing in a hospital. The last thing she seems to remember is talking to me in your driveway. The doctor says she'll probably get more of her memory back, but may not ever remember what happened to her."

"So you don't know who hit her?"

"Nope. It wasn't that much of a blow, though. But it must have thrown her against the gas meter at the side of the house and she hit her head on it and apparently snapped her wrist trying to break her fall. At least, that's what the emergency-room people speculated. They were a lot more concerned with her temperature. She must have laid there in the cold for several hours. If she hadn't been wearing a hat and gloves and a heavy coat, she'd have probably died of exposure."

"Do you think that means whoever it was didn't mean to kill her?" Jane asked.

"Whatever the original intention was, she was left to die. It comes to the same thing as far as I'm concerned. If you hadn't peered out the window and seen her, she would have."

"Is this a tribute to what you call my snooping?"

He smiled. "I guess it is. It saved Ginger's life."

While he was feeling mellow and benevolent, Jane needed to ask something else. "What about the computer disk I found? Have the people in your office read it yet?"

"Nope. There are files on it, but they're password protected. They're going to have to get help from the F.B.I. probably. They have super-duper computers that can run through thousands of combinations of letters and numbers until they hit on the right one."

Jane poured another half a cup of coffee and debated

with herself for a few seconds. "'Guardian,'" she said.

"What?"

"'Guardian' is the password."

"How the hell would you know that?" Mel asked. He held up his hand. "No, wait. I'll bet you made a copy of that disk before you gave it to me. Am I right? I should have known! Jane, that was evidence. You had no business messing with it!"

"It wasn't evidence while it was just an unidentified disk in my house," she said. "It was just an unfamiliar . . . thing."

"You know the law on this? Never mind. How did you figure out the password?"

"Shelley and I figured it out rationally. It's our secret."

Jane wouldn't have thought it was possible for human features to express both gratitude and irritation at the same time, but Mel managed it. He went to the kitchen phone and dialed his office. "Harry? Try the word 'guardian' on that disk. Just a hunch." He winked at Jane. "Right. I'll wait. A foreign language? What language? Find someone who recognizes it. Okay, I'll call back."

He hung up and stared at Jane. "Why didn't you tell me that part?"

"You didn't give me the chance. I sent a piece of it to my father though. He'll know. Stay here. I'll show you the printout of the files."

"The printout of the files," Mel groaned. "Are you

setting up your own annex to the police department?"

"I might, if I had the extra space," Jane said over her shoulder as she went to the living room to fetch her papers.

Mel studied the sheets. "Looks Eastern European to me. But then I don't know anything except enough Spanish to order a dinner and a few obscene French phrases."

"Oops, your toast's gone cold. I forgot it." Jane put in two more slices while Mel continued to peruse the papers she'd handed him.

"Have you remembered anything else Ginger said when she was talking to you last night?" Mel asked.

"I told you the whole thing then. She wanted to interview me, I said no. She asked if the police had found the disk and I told her no again. I didn't think I should have told anyone and wasn't positive it was the right disk anyway. I feel bad about that now."

"Why? You did exactly the right thing," Mel said.

"But she was probably over in the Johnsons' yard looking for it when she was attacked. If she'd known it had been found, nothing would have happened to her."

"You can't know that, Jane. Someone may have been following and watching her and would have cornered her somewhere eventually."

"Was there any physical evidence in the Johnsons' yard? A bloody glove or anything like that?"

Mel frowned. "There is one odd thing. Footprints, we think."

"You think?"

"It's hard to tell. We must have stepped on every inch of the snow yesterday while we were raking it up. The whole yard is footprints. But there are a couple strange ones near where Ginger was."

"Strange in what way? Big, little? Pigeon-toed?"

"Big. And more rectangular than most shoes."

"Something foreign? Ethnic boots of some sort? Aren't traditional Japanese shoes sort of rectangular? Is there a sole pattern?"

"Not much. This is such a light, dry snow that it just packs into the pattern after a step or two. One of my men thinks he can see a row of diamond shapes in one of the prints, but I think he has too good an imagination."

"But you think these weird shoe prints belong to her attacker?"

"They could. Or somebody could have just been prowling around earlier."

Bruce Pargeter came up from the basement with an assortment of tools bulging out of a large, beat-up toolbox. "You're all done, Mrs. Jeffry. Try running the water in the guest bathroom. Let it run for a while."

Mel excused himself from plumbing matters and left. Jane noticed that he took her printouts of Lance's computer disk with him. No matter, she could print them out again. Mel hadn't thought to ask her to turn over her copy.

"Bruce, give me a bill right away and let's sit down

and talk about redoing that bathroom," Jane said, back in fully domestic mode.

After Bruce had outlined his ideas for redoing the bathroom, which all sounded good, especially considering that Jane had no ideas of her own in the matter, he left. She'd considered trying to keep him there and chat about the murder and the attack on Ginger, but had an eerie feeling that she shouldn't. It was as if she'd had her quota of good luck in finding things out and if she pushed it any harder, she might get in trouble of some sort. She didn't want to know more about it—she wanted the police to solve it and let her occupy her mind with celebrating the holidays.

She checked the computer for return E-mail from her father, but there was nothing but a spam ad from somebody called "HotChick" saying if the recipient of the note would send $29.95 to a post office box address, a complete guide to curing impotence would be forthcoming.

Jane hit the delete button. She used to send irate responses to junk like this, but it was fruitless.

She wrapped the last of the presents, prepared a new grocery list, and hit the mall. By the time she got home, she was nearly asleep on her feet. She checked E-mail again, found none, and decided she really needed a good nap. Not a few minutes of sleep on the sofa, but a real turn-off-the-phone, get-in-bed nap. She set sandwich makings on the kitchen counter and told the kids she wasn't to be disturbed for any reason for at least two hours.

This unusual request must have alarmed the kids, she realized three hours later. While she slept, they had cleaned the house, even their own rooms. Katie had consulted some cookbooks and was preparing chicken soup. Mike had shoveled the entire driveway and put out the trash and recycle bins for tomorrow morning's pickup. Todd had washed, dried, and brushed Willard, who was now so staticky that he looked like a big yellow tumbleweed.

"Good heavens!" she exclaimed. "All this because I took a nap?"

"We thought you were sick and wanted everything nice for you," Katie said.

"That's very sweet of you all," Jane said. "But I was just tired. Now I feel great."

And she did. Amazing what a little sleep could do.

"You don't want chicken soup?" Katie asked.

"Why don't we all have it with dinner?"

This settled and the kids reassured that she wasn't ill, Jane checked her E-mail again. This time there was a note from her father saying the Jeffry family's Christmas packages had arrived in good order and that her peculiar note wasn't a foreign language. *Change each consonant to the one that comes before it,* his note said. *Same with the vowels. Who is Julianne Newton and why does anybody care if she was a stripper in college and might have been a prostitute? You aren't involved in another murder, are you? Your mother worries. Love, Dad.*

Twenty-three

Even the knowledge of the code didn't help much. Jane phoned Mel with her father's information, then went over to Shelley's.

"My dad broke the code. Where are the printouts?" she said.

Shelley shoved a pair of cake pans, half full of a pink batter, into the oven and ran to get her paperwork. They ended up having to write the alphabet down to keep the letters straight, but quickly had the files deciphered.

Jane looked over the results. "For all the trouble this has been, there's not much of a payoff, is there?"

"I certainly expected something juicier," Shelley agreed.

Most of the notes were extremely sketchy. About a stockbroker down the street, Lance only gave the name of the man's firm and a remark about possible inside trading. Jane's said, *Jeffry pharmacies? Work there? Ask customers about mistakes.* Shelley's said, *Paul Nowack. Polish, but Greek food. Check with random health inspectors.*

"This looks like nothing at all," Jane said.

"I'm going to call Julie and ask if she was a stripper," Shelley said. "Hers is one of the more specific and I'm curious to know if there's any truth whatsoever to it."

"You're sure you want to do that? If she was, she's ashamed of it. Her husband works for a bank. They're pretty stuffy, you know."

"Maybe twenty years ago something like that would have mattered. But nobody takes stuff like that seriously, unless it's a politician or public figure."

Julie didn't seem to be offended. "I wasn't a stripper, I was a go-go dancer. Not many clothes, but some. Why on earth are you asking?"

Shelley didn't have an answer ready and just said, "I'll tell you later." She repeated what Julie had said to Jane. "If she was upset about being asked, she sure didn't show it," Shelley added.

They went back to the list. *Bruce Pargeter—same as Pargeter in KY. Asked around for home repair recommendations. No complaints.*

"Poor old Lance, striking out everywhere," Jane said.

Sam Dwyer's file only said, *Florida. Child.*

There wasn't a file for Sharon Wilhite. Presumably anything he knew about her was in his head and didn't require notes.

The rest were all people who didn't appear to have any involvement with his murder. Some had left the neighborhood long ago. Several were people who had been absolutely proven to be out of town at the time of the murder.

"I'm really disappointed," Jane said. "He didn't really know much of anything about anybody. It was all bluff and speculation."

Shelley shook her head. "Maybe. But then he could have just kept some of these notes as reminders of what he did know. And there might be other disks someplace with more detail."

Jane stood up. "I'm going home. I'm sick of this and starting to feel like I just don't care who killed the jerk and why. I'm going to quit thinking about it and enjoy the holidays."

"Lucky for us that we can just put it aside," Shelley said. "Poor Mel can't."

"I know. But we can't solve every case for him."

Shelley laughed. "I'm going to tell him you said that!"

"Don't you dare!"

Jane was so firmly resolved to stop thinking about the murder that she almost succeeded. She fixed a nice family dinner to go with Katie's chicken soup. She read a couple chapters of a mystery that she thought was too easy to solve, but discovered that her solution had been wrong all along. She tried out a new rinse on her hair that turned out fairly well, but did some serious damage to one of her favorite towels. She found some Static Guard to spray on Willard as the kids had discovered that petting him in the dark generated sparks. She called and had a conversation with Uncle Jim about Christmas dinner, then girded herself to call her sister. Marty, fortunately, was just getting ready to go out to a party and Jane felt blessed indeed that they didn't have to talk very long. Still, Marty managed to make three irritating comments and two downright stupid remarks.

As she went upstairs to bed, she reminded Todd that he had to get up fairly early the next morning.

"Why?"

"Have you forgotten? Pet got those tickets to some Christmas movie that's opening at ten."

Todd was torn. He wanted to see the movie, but didn't want to have to drag Pet along. Jane pointed out that the tickets were scarce and he hadn't managed to bag his own—Pet had, and it was *she* dragging *him* along.

Jane went to bed early, slept like a rock, and was wide awake by seven—with nothing to do. She could hardly remember a time when she didn't have at least the tail end of a "to do" list pending. She let the pets outside, let them back in and fed them. This always had to be done early on Tuesdays because the trash trucks came later in the morning, terrifying the cats and moving Willard to bark his fool head off. Jane went back to bed with a new mystery book that was already overdue at the library. But she couldn't quite get into it.

She was as twitchy today as Julie Newton always was. Maybe that was Julie's problem—she got too much sleep. She tried picturing Julie as a go-go dancer. It wasn't hard. Go-go dancing, as Jane recalled, was all twitching.

Had Julie told Shelley the truth? Even if Julie really had been a stripper and Lance had proof, could it be a reason to kill him? As deep, dark secrets went, it wasn't a very good one.

The only person on the files who appeared to really have something to fear from Lance was Bruce Pargeter. And he freely admitted that he despised the man. And he really didn't have a good alibi for the night Lance was killed. He and his mother were both at home, but she was upstairs and he was in the basement. Even if she had suspected that Bruce had left the house, she certainly wouldn't have let on. He was her son. And the man who was murdered had been largely responsible for her own husband's death.

Jane had the sense that something was stirring around furtively at the back of her brain. Did her subconscious know something it was refusing to let go of? Or was she just hyper because she'd gotten too much sleep?

At nine, she woke Todd and called Mel. "Anything new?" she asked.

"Not a thing except that the files on the disk were a bust, which I guess you know."

"Boring, aren't they." She told him about Shelley's phone conversation with Julie Newton.

"Yes, Julie called earlier. There was something in the paper this morning about the disk having been found and she put two and two together."

"How did the newspaper find out?"

"We told them. And emphasized that we felt there was nothing of use to the investigation on it. I didn't want anybody else bashed around in pursuit of the damned thing. And Ginger is doing well," he added. "She still can't remember what happened to her, but her health is much improved."

"That's good to hear."

"You sound preoccupied," Mel said.

"I am. There's something on the fringe of my mind I can't get a hold on. Something about the attack on Ginger."

"The method? The place? The time?" Mel tried to help her prod the memory.

"No. Never mind. It's probably something useless anyway. How's Addie?"

"Fine. Fine!" he said with exaggerated enthusiasm. "A little bored, of course. I'd hoped to be free more of the time while she was visiting."

She hoped he wasn't hinting that Jane entertain her, but if so, it was a doomed hope. "Well, I better get along. I'm taking Todd and Pet to the premier of a movie. I hope it's something appropriate, but I'm not going to investigate it too thoroughly for fear it's not."

"I'm sure Sam Dwyer has checked it out," Mel said. "He's very protective of his daughter."

"True. You've relieved my mind. Call me later, okay?"

Mel lowered his voice. "Want to see if we can sneak away this afternoon?"

She knew what he had in mind and it sounded good to her, but it wasn't possible. "I have to go back into hostess mode this afternoon and fix a nice dinner. My in-laws are coming over."

"I'm not crazy about celibacy."

"Neither am I, but I've got kids all over my house, you've got your mother at yours and I'm sure every hotel in the city is full of visiting relatives. Talk to you later."

Jane took the kids to the movie. It was nice being able to back out of a pristine driveway, but she wished Mike had set the trash farther to the left. She had no room to avoid falling in the infamous pothole. "Mom!" Todd said, rubbing his head where he'd bumped it on the window. "You've got to get that fixed."

When she got back from dropping them off, Katie was in the kitchen, rummaging in the fridge. "What are you looking for?" Jane asked.

"Eggs. I want scrambled eggs. With bacon."

"I'll fix it," Jane said.

"You will?"

"I've got a lot of extra energy to expend." Jane gestured at Katie to sit down at the table. Jane pulled out a carton of eggs and put them on the counter. Oops, that was the full carton. She thought that there was another with only two eggs left. She found the other carton hiding behind a bowl of cookie dough that had somehow been forgotten. Jane stood for a moment, staring at the egg cartons.

"Mom? What's wrong? Mom? Wake up."

Jane turned to Katie. "Egg cartons," she said. "Egg cartons and milk cartons."

"What are you—"

"Don't talk for a second. Let me think," Jane said. She put the eggs down, mumbling to herself and nodding. "Yes, yes. It has to be. It's the only thing— Katie, I take back my offer to make breakfast."

She ran upstairs, closed the bedroom door behind her and dialed Shelley. In broken phrases, she told Shelley what she'd figured out. "Does that make any sense at all?" she asked.

"It might not be right, but it all fits. But you better call Mel right away. The trash trucks are coming."

"Oh! Yes."

She called Mel, horrified that he might not be at his desk, that the evidence was going to disappear any second. It was plain good luck that he picked up the phone. She ran through her theory again. "Oh, come on, Jane!" he said. "It's all speculation."

"But you can check on one part of it easily. And you better do it fast. The trash trucks are coming," she said, echoing Shelley's warning.

He didn't even say good-bye before hanging up. He *had* taken her seriously in spite of the absurdity of her thoughts.

Shelley was already at the door when Jane got downstairs. Katie was cooking eggs and looking at Jane as if she'd gone bonkers. Jane threw on her coat and boots and she and Shelley went out to the driveway.

Wringing her hands, Jane said, "Should we go steal the trash?"

"No, we could really screw things up if we did that."

As they spoke, a police car turned the corner and stopped at the end of the block. Jane could hear the clank and rumble of trucks on the next street. Mel's MG skidded around the same corner and came to rest pointing the wrong way on the opposite curb. He got out to talk to the other officer, and glancing up the street, made an "OK" sign at Jane.

The trash truck arrived a moment later. The big, ugly blue machine came slowly, belching black fumes and making a clanking racket. Two trash collectors, who had been clinging to the sides, jumped down and headed for the recycle bins. Mel spoke to them. They shook their heads. He spoke again. One of them made to pick up a bin, but Mel stepped in front of him. The driver climbed down and marched over, beefy hands on hips.

Jane and Shelley started to move down the block to get close enough to hear. Mel pulled out a badge. The driver kept arguing and tried to pick up a bin. The other officer tried to stop him. There was a short tussle and the trash driver got back in the truck, making an obscene gesture. The truck moved on.

Mel called to Jane. She and Shelley nearly ran to his summons.

"You took the kids to the movies already, right?"

"Half an hour ago."

"Good. I wouldn't like to have to arrest Sam Dwyer in front of his daughter."

Twenty-four

"Poor little Pet," Julie Newton said, swinging her leg as she sat on one of Jane's kitchen chairs. "How's she taking it?"

Jane was loading the dishwasher. "Well. Much, much too well. Very stoic. She's upstairs with Todd, building a new gadget for the hamster cage as if there were nothing wrong. I'm really worried about her."

Dinner was over. Thelma had gone home, satisfied that the extra child at the family Christmas Eve dinner was with them because her father was ill. Everybody else knew the truth, but it was agreed among them that Thelma would ooze sympathy from every pore and probably drive poor Pet around the bend if she knew about Sam. The weather had turned warmer, but it was foggy, which made the Christmas lights on the houses along the block seem misty and blurred.

"How on earth did you figure out that it was Sam Dwyer? He seemed like such a nice man. So devoted to his daughter."

"Too devoted," Jane said. "His marriage was falling apart, he didn't approve of his frivolous, fun-loving wife, but was apparently afraid she'd divorce him and keep Pet. Mothers usually do get custody. So before it could happen, he kidnapped Pet, moved away, and told Pet her mother had died."

"But how did you know that? How did you even guess?"

"She's psychic," Shelley said, coming in from the living room where she'd been watching Christmas Mass from the Vatican on the television.

"No, really," Julie insisted.

"It was the egg cartons first," Jane said. "Mel had described some footprints that were found near Ginger's body. He said they were blurry and rectangular. It sounded like some kind of weird shoes or boots. But I wondered at the time why somebody who obviously didn't want to be identified would deliberately wear footgear that was so easily identifiable. Then, this morning I was holding two egg cartons and it suddenly occurred to me that you could tape them to your feet, then just put them back into the trash and nobody would ever associate them with shoes. Which is exactly what Sam did. Some of the duct tape he used to keep them on his feet was still on them."

"But why did you think of Sam? We all have egg cartons," Julie persisted.

"Because I'd seen them in his recycling bin when we went there for dinner. That's the only reason he even crossed my mind. But egg cartons made me think of milk cartons. Pet told me she had to drink special milk. I tasted hers at her house and it tasted exactly like the ordinary milk you get in paper cartons."

"Because it was," Shelley added.

"I don't get it yet," Julie said.

"It wasn't the milk that was different," Jane explained. "It was the container."

Julie thought for a minute, then her eyes opened very wide. "They have pictures of missing children on them!"

"Right. And Sam didn't dare risk Pet ever seeing her name or one of those 'age-enhanced' pictures on a milk carton," Shelley said.

"I still could have been badly wrong," Jane said. "It was all just mental leaping around. But it gave Mel what he needed. He immediately contacted the missing-children people in Florida. It literally only took seconds because Sam hadn't even attempted to change his name. He just took Pet and left one day while his wife was at the grocery store."

"We should have realized something had changed when he wanted to be invited to the cookie party," Shelley said.

"Right," Jane said. "He hadn't wanted anything to do with the neighbors until then. I'd invited him to the caroling party and he didn't even respond, much less show up. Then suddenly the next day, he wants to be involved in neighborhood activities."

"And wanted to be chummy with you in particular," Shelley said.

Jane made a face at her. "What's so weird about that?"

"You've been here in the neighborhood all this time, but as soon as Lance King was killed right next door to you after being in your house, he's suddenly interested in you. That's what's weird."

"And I thought it was my charm," Jane said.

"Has Sam admitted to the murder?" Julie asked.

Jane nodded. "He went to pieces, Mel told me. Said he'd dreaded losing Pet all these years. He was obsessed with it. He feared everybody who asked him about himself was a private detective. And when he heard Lance King was coming to the neighborhood, he was worried. Then Lance did that piece on the news about the 'dirty underbelly of life in the suburbs' or whatever it was, and he was horrified that Lance knew about Pet. It was sheer panic, I imagine, that made him come up here and watch to see if Lance left the house between broadcasts. And, unfortunately for both of them, that's just what Lance did."

"Did Lance know about Sam and Pet?" Shelley asked.

"I don't imagine we'll ever know," Jane said. "But my guess is that he did. Mel says there's a perfect view of the Dwyer house from the Johnsons' roof. No trees or fences in the way. And it had to be someone on the opposite side of the street he was watching."

"And what about that reporter?" Julie asked.

"Apparently he just stumbled onto her by accident. He had no idea she was there, and nearly ran into her. Then he really panicked and ran home."

"So he didn't have the egg cartons on his feet to keep him from being identified as the person who hit her?"

"I don't think so. I think he was just afraid the police

might come back and see strange footprints and ask him what he'd been looking for," Jane said.

"I know what he did was awful," Julie said, tapping her fingertips on the table. "But it was only because he loved his daughter so much that he did those awful things."

Shelley said, "But he didn't do it for Pet, really. He did it for himself. To keep her to himself and away from her mother. I suppose he thought that was in Pet's best interests, but still, it wasn't right to steal the child and then kill someone to keep from being discovered."

Jane poured them all some coffee and sat down where she could see out the front window. "Pet is twelve years old. Almost thirteen. Sam told Mel that if she'd been sixteen, he wouldn't have done anything. He thought the 'window' for losing her ended then because even if he were found out, she'd have the legal choice of deciding which parent to stay with."

"And he didn't doubt she'd choose him?" Julie asked.

"How could he doubt it?" Shelley said. "Sam was the only parent she knew or remembered."

"I'm not so sure," Jane said. "She remembers her mother vividly, or thinks she does."

Jane caught a flash of light outside and looked out the window. A police car had pulled into the driveway. Jane motioned to Shelley and Julie to stay put. Then she went to the front door, opened it, and waited.

The woman who came to the door looked much like

she had in the photograph album. Older, of course. And a bit thinner. Less flamboyant. And very, very nervous.

"I'm Patty Sue Dwyer," she said.

"I know you are," Jane said with a smile. "I've never been happier to meet anyone. I thought you might want to meet with Pet privately. Come up to my bedroom and I'll send her to you."

"What if she hates me?" Patty Sue blurted out. She was very pale in spite of a good Florida tan.

"She won't," Jane assured her.

Jane got Patty Sue settled in her bedroom and closed the door, then went to Todd's room. He was still fiddling with the hamster gadget. Pet was sitting on the edge of the bed. Her hands were folded neatly in her lap, and her gaze was fixed blankly on the opposite wall.

"Pet?" Jane said.

Pet turned to her slowly, her eyes behind her goggly glasses bleak.

"I have something for you. Come to my room with me."

Pet followed obediently. Jane opened the door and Pet stepped in. Patty Sue stood perfectly still and said, "Oh, Pet. My darling Pet."

Pet was frozen in place. She stared and blinked owlishly. Then she whispered, "Mommy!" and ran to fling herself into her mother's waiting arms.

Christmas morning dawned bright and clear, the sun

sparkling on what remained of the snow. It was the one day of the year that the kids wanted to get up early. There had always been a rule, however, that they couldn't come downstairs until nine o'clock. They were lined up like racehorses at the starting post at one minute before. Jane and the kids went through the comfortable, comforting routine. Todd distributed the gifts and they opened them one at a time, going from youngest to oldest until everything was opened.

Jane fixed a light breakfast and afterwards, the kids tried on new clothes, checked out their new stuff, and Jane indulged herself in playing the adventure game Mike had gotten her for her laptop. At noon, Thelma arrived, this time without her son Ted and his wife Dixie. Ted and Dixie spent Christmas Day with Dixie's parents and siblings. Mel and Addie arrived an hour later. Mel looked happy and rested.

"How's Pet doing?" he asked.

"Patty Sue called a few minutes ago and said they were both fine," Jane answered.

"Poor child," Addie said. Apparently Mel had filled her in on the case and its resolution. "Her father going to jail."

"But she has her mother back," Jane said. "That doesn't make it better, exactly, but she needs her mother's influence. If you could have seen her smile when she and her mother came downstairs—" Jane started tearing up again. She'd done that a couple of times since witnessing the reunion and would probably keep on doing so for quite a while. "I have to check the turkey," she said, turning away abruptly.

Mel followed her a minute later and took her into the little hallway leading to the guest bath and garage door. "You're a good woman," he said before kissing her.

"And you're a good man to put up with me," she said.

"I have a gift I want to give you now. I don't know if you want it or not."

He pulled a tiny box out of his pocket and handed it to her. She knew what it was without opening it. But she opened it anyway. It was a diamond ring.

"Oh, Mel—"

"You don't have to answer right now. Just keep it while you're deciding."

A dozen thoughts flashed through her mind. One of the more trivial ones was the concept of having not one, but two mothers-in-law, neither of whom liked her. Another was how much she loved this good man.

"Mel, I have such gifts this year. My kids, my friends, my home, and you."

"But—?"

"But I wish you'd keep this and give it to me again next Christmas . . . if you still want to."

She was afraid he'd be angry—or worse, hurt. Instead, he smiled and put his hand out for the box. "All right. If that's what you want."

Jane took a step back and looked at him severely. "You're *relieved!*"

"No, I'm not!" he said, still smiling.

"You are! I can tell. You're supposed to beg me to change my mind."

"Would you?"

"No."

"Then why should I waste my effort?" He was openly laughing at her now.

She started laughing, too. She snuggled into his arms and said, "I like things just like they are, Mel."

"So do I."

"Mom? Where are you? The gravy's burning," Katie yelled from the kitchen.

"You save the gravy, I'll save this," Jane said, holding up the ring box.

"Promise?" Mel asked.

"I promise."

Center Point Publishing
600 Brooks Road ● PO Box 1
Thorndike ME 04986-0001 USA

(207) 568-3717

US & Canada:
1 800 929-9108